Albert R. Broccoli presents
Pierce Brosnan
as Ian Fleming's James Bond 007 in

GOLDENEYE

with Sean Bean, Izabella Scorupco, Famke Janssen and
Joe Don Baker

Associate Producer	Anthony Waye
Editor	Terry Rawlings
Music	Eric Serra
Director of Photography	Phil Meheux
Production Designer	Peter Lamont
Executive Producer	Tom Pevsner
Written by	Michael France and Jeffrey Caine
Produced by	Michael G Wilson and Barbara Broccoli
Directed by	Martin Campbell

More James Bond Novels by John Gardner

Licence Renewed
For Special Services
Icebreaker
Role of Honour
No Deals Mr Bond
Nobody Lives For Ever
Scorpius
Win, Lose or Die
Brokenclaw
The Man From Barbarossa
Death is Forever
Never Send Flowers
SeaFire

Licence to Kill
(based on the film written by
Michael G. Wilson and Richard Maibaum)

Ian Fleming's

JAMES BOND

in
John Gardner's

Based on the screenplay by Michael France
and Jeffrey Caine

Hodder & Stoughton

Contents

1 Cowslip – 1986   1
2 Mission Accomplished   11
3 High Stakes   23
4 The Spider and the Admiral   33
5 The Tigre's A Wonderful Thing   43
6 Petya   53
7 EMP   67
8 Assignment GoldenEye   77
9 Wade's Ten Cent Tour   89
10 Wheeling and Dealing   105
11 The God with Two Faces   119
12 Floating Through Sunlight   129
13 Track Event   141
14 The Train   153
15 Steel-Plated Coffin   163
16 Interlude   173
17 The Lake   189
18 The Edge of Catastrophe   197
19 Journeys End in Lovers Meeting   209

1

Cowslip – 1986

His head seemed to explode. He felt the great roar in his ears, the pounding of blood, then the sensation that his skull was riddled with holes. Fire poured through the holes, from his ears and nostrils, then his mouth. James Bond jerked awake, realising several things at once. The roar came from two Soviet jets, afterburners guzzling fuel as they passed overhead. He recalled that, at the briefing, they had said military jets often flew low over the mountains heading back to their base near Russia's oldest sea port, Archangel.

He also cursed himself for falling from a doze into a deep sleep. He stretched, trying to ease his aching muscles, then moved very slowly to glance at his watch. It was nearly time to go and he was cold and suffering from cramps. He listened and could still hear the jets receding but no sound of the spotter aircraft which used the airfield far below.

The spotter plane was over sixty years old – a Fiesler Storch captured at Stalingrad from Hitler's Luftwaffe. To watch it would be like seeing an old Roman ballista on the electronic battlefield of the 1980s.

Wide awake now, Bond looked around, alert, becoming orientated. He lay at the top of a high ridge within the bowl surrounded by dark hostile mountains. To his right was the long man-made lake and in front of him the squat concrete guardhouse blocking entry to the top of the vast dam which rose some eight hundred feet from the valley floor.

Below the dam, the ground was a mass of boulders and rocks, but he knew these were only camouflage for they were cemented into almost twenty feet of bomb proof stressed concrete and steel. Beneath those rocks lay the target: BioChemical Processing Plant Number One.

In spite of the 1972 convention, the Soviets had gone on making biological and chemical warheads deep under the earth in this bleak place.

Until now, M had told them, the manufacture was confined to known horrors: anthrax and a number of nerve and more conventional gases, but now the place was being retooled to produce something far more deadly – one of the many viruses which were being isolated as man slowly destroyed the world's rain forests. Within a couple of weeks, the underground factory would be capable of producing a biological agent which was the stuff of nightmares: a fast-spreading virus capable of thinning the blood of its victims, rapidly breaking down the human body so that one by one the main organs would shut down. This was a quick, though terrifying, death.

The Soviets at least had to be slowed down, if not stopped altogether from producing warheads and bomblets containing this catastrophic agent. M had been clear about the urgency. The West needed time to work on some form of immunisation, and it was down to James

Bond, 007, and his old friend Alec Trevelyan, 006, to get the job done.

'You are my two best men,' the Old Man had said, 'and we're all aware that this operation gives you only a fifty-fifty chance of return. But I have no other option. The place must be destroyed now. Another few weeks and it'll be too late.'

In the here and now, Bond turned his head and looked down into the valley, reflecting on the repulsive nature of the work going on beneath the brutal earth in this godforsaken bleak area in the far north of the Soviet empire.

The only visible sign of life below him was the rough runway which scarred the ground, like an open wound, ending only about thirty feet from the edge of a long gorge which ran parallel to the dam, at the far end of the plateau above the valley floor. The gorge was around a mile wide and very deep, with its own valley floor.

The runway, they had been told, was one of the two ways in and out of the processing plant. Workers, security troops and scientists were flown in and out using an old Antonov An-14 Bee which had been modified and given a VSTOL (Very Short Take Off and Landing) capability.

The other entrance and exit was by a crude underground railway, cut in the late 1960s through earth and rock, enabling personnel and product to be linked with the port of Archangel. The rolling stock of this unsophisticated transport system consisted mainly of flatbed cars to carry products, and open carriages with hardwood seats for staff and troops. The journey from Archangel to the processing plant took almost twenty-four hours – a day of intense discomfort.

Alec Trevelyan had been inserted three days before into Archangel itself, and, if all the documents were in order and nobody had questioned his cover, he should by now have made the long underground journey into the processing plant itself.

M had seen it as a two-handed job. Trevelyan was to get in and provide an entrance through one of the grilles set into the thick roof, close to an air conditioning unit. Inside he was also charged with preparing a safe zone from which he and Bond could operate.

Bond's task was to take out the two guards at their post on top of the dam, then to carry the arms and explosives down to Trevelyan. They were then to blast the secret facility to hell and make their way back to an extraction point some twenty miles east of Archangel. Nobody concerned had any doubts as to the near suicidal nature of the operation. *Operation Cowslip*. Bond gave a wry smile at the code name, thinking it singularly inappropriate for what they were to do. There's many a slip twixt cow and lip, he thought, his smile broadening.

Again he stretched his legs and arms. He had been lying in this position, less than fifty yards from the guard post, for over seven hours after being parachuted – using the High Altitude Low Opening (HALO) technique, from a stealth equipped aircraft – eight hours before. He had landed short of his DZ and it had taken an hour to climb the quarter of a mile up the rocky incline leading to the small outcrop of rock which would give him access to the guard post.

The post was simply a square, concrete and steel structure perched on the edge of the dam's top. There was a window and door on Bond's side of the building, and he knew from the briefing photographs that inside there was room for the two permanent guards to eat, relax and sleep. He also knew that on the far side was a kind of enclosed dog pen constructed of high steel bars, with a sliding electronic gate at the end which led out to the walkway on top of the dam itself.

The soldiers who manned this post were part of the security detail on permanent assignment to BioChemical Processing Plant Number One. These were troops drawn from the KGB Border Guards Department, all of whom had undergone special extra training with the élite Spetsnaz troops. The other end of the dam needed no such guards as it abutted straight onto a sheer rock face.

The pair of guards were changed weekly, making a tough and unpleasant climb up a set of wide D-shaped rungs set firmly into the dam's vertical wall. For a second, he wondered what that climb would be like in the bleakest midwinter. Even Bond shuddered at the thought, then, knowing that the time for his own descent was nearing, he mentally checked off the equipment he carried.

He wore a specially designed wet suit, climbing boots and a long parka. The wet suit and parka were both a stone grey colour and contained more zippered and buttoned pockets than you would find in a poacher's greatcoat. In Bond's case, he carried equipment wrapped around his chest under the parka, and a long pocket containing what he hoped would be his ultimate salvation ran down the right thigh of the wet suit. Further, a broad webbing belt was clipped around his waist. At least four pouches were threaded onto the belt, plus a webbing holster for his weapon of choice, the ASP 9mm, loaded with ferocious Glaser ammunition and fitted with a long noise reduction cylinder. His face and head were covered in an insulated ski mask, while his hands were protected by skin-tight leather gloves which kept out the cold without reducing his ability to use his fingers for the most delicate of tasks.

In his head he ticked off the contents of the pockets and pouches, as he had done a dozen times before the cold and fatigue had pushed him into a dangerous sleep.

As he went through the items, Bond became aware of noise, the splutter and buzz of the Storch's engine far away below on the edge of the runway. It was the first signal, for the old spotter aircraft ran regular patrols over the area, its pilot making sure that no civilian climbing enthusiasts, or worse, enemies of the state, had made their way just a shade too close to the restricted area.

The Storch flew a pre-set pattern which seldom varied and took around twenty minutes to complete. Its final manoeuvre was to fly low across the lake, passing over the dam at its midpoint. From the large greenhouse cockpit the pilot would scan the guard post, and routine security required that one of the KGB Border Guards would come out into the steel cage and signal an 'all clear' to the aircraft. In spite of the fact that there was both a two-way radio and a telephone in the guard post, this was the kind of instruction beloved of Colonel Ourumov, the officer in charge of security. Arkady Grigorovich Ourumov, a senior officer of the KGB Border Guards, was well known to Western agents such as Bond. It was said of him that his view of security was so paranoid that should he ever get his way, he would have guards watching guards watching guards, and so on to infinity.

Below, the enigma pitch changed on the Fiesler Storch as it began its take off run. Bond slowly rose, flexing his limbs, then he noiselessly ran towards the building, flattening himself against the wall to the right of the grimy window. As he did so, he was aware of the aircraft climbing out of the valley.

Quickly he leaned inwards, peering through the window. The two soldiers sat opposite one another concentrating on a chess game. What happens, he wondered, if they miss their cue by not signalling to the plane?

The aircraft noise was receding; now he detected another change of engine noise and an increase in sound as, far out over the lake, it began to line up with the centre of the dam.

Pressed against the wall, he clearly heard the guards' voices and the scrape as a chair was pushed back.

Once more he leaned towards the window. One of the men was opening the door on the dam side and walking out into the steel enclosure, the other soldier still sat at the table, his entire concentration on the chess board.

Listening for the aircraft's approach, Bond removed the automatic pistol from its holster and edged towards the door. As he passed the window he could see that the guard outside was shielding his eyes, looking upwards.

In one fluid movement he opened the door, stepped inside the building and lifted his right hand. The man puzzling over the chess board was so engrossed that his reactions were considerably slowed. He turned, looked blankly at Bond as though he were someone from another planet, then began to push his chair back, his face a mixture of surprise, fear, and disbelief.

The automatic made little noise, just a quiet phut-phut. In fact the metallic click of the mechanism seemed louder than the actual rounds being fired. Bond winced slightly as the two Glasers blew into the man's chest, right over the heart, the pair hitting within a quarter of an inch of each other. Overkill, Bond thought as the twin odours of gunsmoke and blood twitched at his nostrils. His lifetime experience taught him to always fire two rounds, in the traditional manner. With Glasers you only needed one, for ninety per cent of victims hit by this round ended up dead within seconds, it being virtually a shotgun cartridge, the No. 12 shot floating in liquid Teflon within a thin cupronickel jacket, the bullet sealed with a plastic cap. It was the sudden outward explosion of the No. 12 shot once the bullet entered the body that did the damage.

The dead soldier's chair had been pushed back, almost to the wall by the impact. Now the body slumped to one side and fell to the floor, one arm flapping against the chess board, scattering the pieces.

The spotter aircraft was passing overhead, and as Bond stepped over the body so the telephone began to ring.

Bond hesitated, a fraction too long, his eyes searching for the incoming point. The telephone rang five times before he reached down and ripped the jack from the socket. By then he heard the other guard running back towards the building. He could hear the man's boots thudding on the paving and could imagine him unholstering his pistol.

'Definitely not officer material,' Bond murmured. The man was just rushing back without even making a tactical appraisal of what might, or might not, be happening inside the guard post. He exploded through the door, the little Stechkin automatic waving, almost out of control, in his hand.

This time, Bond fired only once. The second soldier spun to the left, hit the wall and collapsed, leaving a trail of smeared blood behind him. In the silence that followed, two of the chess pieces rolled at his feet.

'Checkmate,' Bond muttered, taking stock of the situation, looking specifically for the control to the gate out on the top of the dam. The big metal button like an unpolished silver mushroom was set into the wall high to the left of the door, just where they said it would be. He glanced at his watch, seeing there was not much time left. If all had gone smoothly, Alec Trevelyan would be in place waiting for him. The plan had been to set the charge and get out while the bulk of the Plant's staff were on their one hour's mid-morning break.

He unzipped the parka and began to unwind the cumbersome thick elasticised rope from around his body, curling it across his left arm, making certain that the entire length was free and there was no danger of it getting tangled. In the next few minutes his life would depend on the strength and pliability of this piece of equipment which he coiled so that the strengthened noose was in his left hand and the big spring clip in his right. Reaching up, Bond banged the big button which controlled the outer gate, hitting it squarely with the spring clip.

He heard the whine of the metal from the far end of the cage, looked out and saw that the way onto the wide top of the dam was clear. Taking a deep breath he began to sprint forward.

2

Mission Accomplished

He had not anticipated the stiff breeze blowing off the lake, but the top of the dam was wide enough, and there was no question of doing a balancing act as the wind whipped around him. There were strong metal guardrails running along cither sidc, so Bond had no worrics about falling off and hurtling through the eight hundred feet of space onto the rocks below – even though this was basically what he was about to do.

He reached the centre of the high curved structure, glanced down and felt his stomach turn over. In the short period they had been given to prepare for *Operation Cowslip*, he had done this only twice, and then dropping less than half the distance he was about to attempt. You only got one chance with this method, and there were no things like reserve parachutes or wrist clamped altimeters.

Initially he had suggested abseiling down the face of the dam, but quickly realised that this tried and true method would leave him exposed to detection for longer than anyone wanted – including himself.

He banged the spring clip onto one of the metal

guardrail uprights, and gave it a quick pull, quietly hoping
the iron to which he was tethering himself was bedded
firmly into the top of the dam as the experts claimed.
Hardly stopping to think about anything else, Bond slid
his right foot into the noose at the other end of the bungee
cord and pulled the long piton gun – assembled lovingly
by Q's people – from its special holster in the thigh of his
wet suit. Ducking under the rail, he glanced back to be
certain the cord was free of any obstruction, and could
not get tangled. Then, expelling his breath in a loud *whaaa*
sound, James Bond launched himself from the top of the
dam.

This was nothing like free fall parachuting because you
did not have the comfortable knowledge that, when the
moment came, there was a 'chute on your back. Bond's
stomach was still up on top of the dam as he plunged
downwards. The drop seemed endless. He could feel his
body moving faster and even felt the resistance of the air
through which he moved. His ears sang and his facial
muscles ceased to be of any value, his cheeks forced back
and his mouth stretched in what he knew was a kind of
hideous grin.

As he plummeted with the dam's wall only a foot or so
from his body, he pushed the piton gun forward, his hands
firmly holding its twin grips which eventually would be his
way to safety. The use of this piece of equipment had to
be timed to the second. If not, the bungee cord would
reach its maximum length and he would be sprung back,
lifted by the cord then falling again and, in all probability,
smashed into the hard wall of the dam.

Struggling against the pressure, Bond forced himself to
look down at the rocky ground hurtling up to meet him.
He relied solely on instinct to judge the moment to fire
the piton. There was no accurate way of calculating the

optimum second, and he knew that his sense of self-preservation could now easily override accuracy.

Then, right or wrong, the moment was upon him. He clung to the handles of the piton gun as he pressed the trigger and felt the projectile charge thump, the tingling of the small explosion running up his arms. The barbed arrow that was the piton shot down, trailing a snake of around a hundred feet of ultra strong climbing rope behind it, moving with a speed that was a fraction faster than Bond's downward momentum.

The piton smashed into the camouflaged concrete at the foot of the dam at just the moment that the bungee cord had paid out its normal length, but with around two hundred feet of elastation to go. Bond felt the pull and, for a second, thought his arms were going to be torn from their sockets. The muscles of both arms and the right leg screamed pain through him, and he wondered if this had been the kind of thing men first felt on the rack in those days of intense physical torture. He reached forward hand over hand, beginning to haul himself downwards to the bottom of the dam, his face contorted with agony as he fought against the pressure from the bungee cord which was now taut, pulling, trying to drag him back up the dam wall.

Finally Bond reached the bottom, strung between the rope and the thick bungee cord. Looking down, he could see the strain on the piton which was moving slightly in the concrete in which it was embedded.

If the piton was ripped out by tension on the bungee, he was well aware of what could happen: he would be catapulted upwards, against the side of the wall. His body would be scraped as though someone held him against a huge Black & Decker sander. In the end the bungee would leap into the air, eight hundred feet above, and what was left of him would be thrown down onto the top of the dam.

Even now, he felt himself being torn apart by the bungee's tension and the anchored rope around his left arm. He reached up to free his foot from the loop and the bungee shot back up the dam wall, flying upwards like a long fast-moving snake.

He stood for a moment, orientating himself, then moved in a crouch over the rocks, zig-zagging between them to reach the air conditioning pump which stood like a grey painted drum about twenty yards away. The grille, next to the pump, had been opened and he could see the marks where Alec Trevelyan had used a metal-cutting instrument on the big padlock. As he pulled the grille back, Bond found himself looking into a dark square hole with the top elongated D-shape of a series of rungs set in the side of the wall below.

Swinging himself into the darkness, he began to descend, not rushing but moving slowly, his feet feeling out the rungs, his mind focused on finding the bottom of this black well, for he had no idea how far this maintenance shaft went down.

It turned out to be a long haul, for the wide duct seemed to go down forever. Though his eyes were gradually getting used to the blackness, Bond – for the first time in his life – started to experience a kind of vertigo, his senses stretched to the limit. His muscles still ached and his mind felt detached from what he was actually doing. Everything had happened so quickly that a part of him was still high up above the ground, plunging towards the rocks and cement; his hands on the rungs felt bruised and there was a musty damp smell in his nostrils. It was an odour that became stronger the further he moved downward.

After what seemed to be ten or fifteen minutes and

hundreds of metal rungs, his feet touched solid ground. A floor? Or was it a ledge from which he could easily fall into some bottomless pit? By now he had ceased to trust his senses, and his mind became obsessed with heights.

Very slowly he adjusted to the blackness of his surroundings. He appeared to be in some small chamber which he presumed was the access point to the maintenance shaft. To his right, Bond could just make out the shape of a door. His feet scraped loudly on the stone floor as he crossed to the door, gently pulling it open and moving through into what felt like a larger chamber.

Two steps in he stopped, frozen like a statue. He could smell the scent of blood and death. More, he was conscious of the cold metal of a pistol gently resting in his neck, just under his ear.

'Don't even breathe,' a voice said in Russian. Then, 'Where are the others?'

'I'm alone.' His voice a fraction more relaxed.

'Aren't we all?' There was a faint chuckle and the lights came on, almost blinding him with their brightness. He turned to see his old friend, Alec Trevelyan, grinning at him, still looking like the eternal schoolboy. Many had said of Trevelyan that he had a picture in the attic, like Dorian Grey.

'Glad you could drop in, James.'

'It was a slightly longer journey than I'd expected, but most of it was downhill.'

Trevelyan motioned towards a second door, open and revealing a curved metal stairwell.

'You ready, James?'

'Let's do it.' Bond moved first, through the door and down the spiral stairwell. 'You come up this way?' he asked of 006.

'Yes. There's a door at the bottom to your right and

another facing you. That's the one with the electronic locks. Behind it you'll find Aladdin's cave. After a fashion anyway.'

Already Bond was unzipping one of the pouches on his belt. By the time they reached the electronic door he had the little oblong box in his hand. The box was magnetic and he clamped it onto the side of the door, throwing a small switch as he did so. Immediately a series of lights began to pulse and a small digital read-out started to move very fast. 'It's really quite simple,' Q had said. 'It works very like an autodialler, except it sorts through every known permutation of numbers and letters at a speed of around five hundred a second. When it detects part of a matching pattern it starts to configure the entire electronic code. Even on a cleverly invented system it shouldn't take more than fifteen minutes to hit the right numbers or letters. As soon as it's done that, the lock will be activated.'

'A very handy little gadget to take on a picnic,' Bond had replied.

Q had given him the ghost of a smile. 'I had it tested on the vaults below the Bank of England,' he said. 'The people there didn't like it one bit.'

By the time Bond's memory took in the conversation, the box gave a final little beep and the door clicked open.

They were on a high, suspended walkway, looking down on what seemed to be a huge manufacturing plant. On the far side a row of some six massive stainless steel vats stood in line, linked together by slim metal tubing. This line of vats ended in a mass of tubes and pumps which went into a much larger container like some kind of pressure cooker. More tubes and pumps disappeared through the wall area to their right. By this time, Bond was completely disoriented. He had no idea of his position in relation to the ground above.

To the left, at the end of these gigantic containers was another electronic door, while directly underneath them Bond could make out a wide conveyor belt, running the length of the floor and rolling through a fringed rubber flap.

'What's through there?' Bond indicated the electronic door.

'The rest of the laboratories, I should think.' Trevelyan gave another chuckle. 'I just went missing into the connecting passages when I got here. The map M gave us was pretty accurate, so I hid up where you found me. I played at being a kind of phantom of the labs so to speak. The music of the night down here isn't really my thing though.'

Bond indicated the big red signs, decorated with skulls and crossed bones which hung everywhere. In Russian they said: 'DANGER. HIGHLY INFLAMMABLE.' 'And those?' he asked.

'They're scouring out all the equipment. I gathered, from what I heard on that quite disgusting underground train ride, that this is all new stuff. Has to be absolutely clean before they start processing the new horror.'

'Smoking in here could seriously damage your health then?'

'Definitely, and the second-hand smoke would kill very quickly indeed.'

'Let's get the place rigged up.' Bond headed towards the steps that led down onto the deadly factory's floor and clamped the electronic device onto the door at the end. Then he began emptying his pouches and pockets of the neatly packaged timers and charges which he had carried in with him.

Together they set about placing the explosives behind the vats and on the connecting tubing.

'I'll do the last one,' he called to Trevelyan. 'If I

set it for three minutes or so that should give us plenty of time to get out. The rest'll go up by spontaneous combustion. . . .'

The device on the door gave its final little beep, signifying that it had unlocked the electronic password, and as it did so a piercing, shrieking warning klaxon went off.

Bond swore. 'Get behind this stuff, Alec. No time to . . .' He was cut off by the sound of a voice, magnified by an electric loud hailer –

'This is Colonel Ourumov,' the disembodied voice grated. 'You are surrounded and there is no way you can escape. Just drop any weapons and come out with your hands on your heads. Now!'

'No way,' Bond muttered, continuing down the line of steel vats that towered above him. Aloud he called, 'Alec, put that bit of high-tech gadgetry into reverse. Just hit the switch on the left side.'

He had almost reached the final high pressure cooker device. 'Alec?' He ducked down and peered around the corner of the drum.

His old friend 006, Alec Trevelyan, knelt on the floor. Behind him, with the muzzle of a pistol against Trevelyan's cheek, stood a tall, sinister Soviet officer wearing the shoulder boards of a colonel. He was backed by half-a-dozen heavily armed troops, one of whom loosed off a round in Bond's direction.

'Fool. Stop that,' yelled Ourumov. 'If you hit any of the hardware, you'll blow us all to hell and gone.'

Bond drew back, and looked at the timer he was about to insert into the final charge, the one that would bring about a chain reaction and blow most of the place to pieces. He glanced across to the other side of the factory floor towards the conveyor belt. The start button was set into a metal post near the fringed rubber flap.

'I give you a count of ten,' Ourumov shouted. 'If you're not out by then, I will shoot your comrade.'

'And set off an inferno?' Bond set the timer for one minute and plugged it into the explosive charge. Then he removed a grenade from the belt pouch that contained four of these lethal little bombs.

'One . . . Two . . .' Ourumov began counting.

Bond pulled the pin from the grenade, holding down the safety lever.

'Three . . . Four. . . .'

Bond stepped from behind the massive steel pressure cooker. His arms were wide apart, the grenade in his left hand, pistol in the right.

'Five. . . .'

'You kill him, we all die.' Bond knew that was pretty near the truth. Apart from the grenade, the main charge would blow in about thirty seconds.

'You think I'm not afraid to die for my country?' Ourumov snapped. Then he pulled the trigger and Bond saw his old friend topple over.

Without a second thought he dropped the grenade, leaped to his right onto the conveyor belt, his free hand smacking the start button on the metal upright.

He heard Ourumov yell at his men to hold their fire, and thought he saw him backing away, dragging Trevelyan's body with him.

The conveyor belt started to move with a jerk and, now that he was away from the vats and cylinders filled with inflammable cleaning fluids, the Russian colonel fired two shots. The bullets smacked into the woodwork above the rubber skirt just as the belt carried Bond out of the pro-cessing room, angling upwards and moving fast.

The grenade exploded with an earshattering blast. He thought he could hear screams, then, suddenly, he found

19

himself being deposited onto a loading bay, outside the facility, only some fifty yards from the runway where the little Fiesler Storch was slowly taxiing, its tail towards him, ready to make the ninety-degree turn onto the threshold for take off.

The first explosion came from deep within the earth behind him, almost throwing him forward onto the unfriendly ground. Nobody was going to get out of the complex alive, that was a sure bet, so he began to run, heading towards the aircraft.

With bursting lungs, Bond reached it just as it started to turn and begin rolling. Behind him another explosion. This time a blossom of flame, smoke and debris seemed to erupt from the ground. He leaped forward, catching the wing strut on the right hand side of the Storch. The pilot, concentrating on keeping the aircraft straight as it began to gather speed, glanced towards him and retarded the power, trying to abort the take off, as Bond reached out to the handle on the cockpit door.

The pilot, hitting the brakes to slow the plane, banged the rudder to the left, making the Storch yaw violently in an attempt to throw Bond from the wing strut, but when that did not work, he opened the door on his side and rolled from the cockpit, pushing the throttle to full power as he went.

With a push, Bond catapulted himself from the strut to the right hand seat, then leaned over to ease back on the throttle as he pulled himself across to get behind the controls.

The aircraft was turning in a wide circle, out of control, bumping along the rough ground, lurching and dipping first one wing and then the other, leaving Bond in no doubt that it would cartwheel any second. He snatched back on the throttle, pressed the rudder pedals to gain control and, as another explosion fountained behind him, he swung the nose onto the runway, fishtailing violently until the Storch pointed down the centre line.

He was almost two thirds of the way down the runway and at a standstill, desperately looking around the cockpit to acclimatise himself with the controls when he felt the plane being rocked violently by another explosion.

Bond pulled down on the flaps lever and saw that the wide extensions to the trailing edge of the wings became fully extended. As they did so, he opened the throttle to full power and moved his feet back, easing off the brakes on the rudder pedals.

The Storch leaped forward, gathering speed, and eating up what was left of the runway. He felt the tail come up as the machine reached the end of the metalled section and bounced over the twenty odd yards of turf, heading straight for the long wide crevasse. Even with flaps fully extended, Bond knew he had not quite made enough speed to lift the Storch into the air. He eased back on the stick and felt the aircraft claw for its natural element. It rolled off the end of the solid ground, hung in midair for a second, before the nose dropped as she stalled and began to lose height, falling into the deep fissure.

He saw the rock face rising on both sides, great boulders and a stream less than two hundred feet below, getting closer with each second. Gently he eased off on the power, tilted the straining aircraft to the left, lifting the nose slightly so that he could gain enough airspeed for the plane's wings to take over the weight.

It seemed an eternity before he could ease back, and feel the nose come right up, the whole machine stabilising. Slowly he began to climb from the gorge and turn back over the facility which was now rubble and fire leaping from under the ground.

As he climbed away, Bond thought he saw the dam begin to split and crack, spilling water across the entire valley. It was no time to feel any sentiment. Alec Trevelyan had taken the same risks as anyone else in the Double-O Section. If not for a twist of fate, it could have been himself down there, shot through the head, his body being slowly covered by the water that was now crashing white from the lake.

Flying as low as he dared, Bond began to play tag with the mountains as he steadily made his way back to the area where in a matter of hours a submarine would take him back to England with *Operation Cowslip* successfully accomplished. On reflection, the one thing that pleased him was the fact that there had been no biological or chemical weapons actually in the complex. If there had been, the idea of blowing the place up was just about as foolish a concept as you could have. So, he presumed, M had already known there was little likelihood of deadly germs or toxic chemicals at the plant.

There was no way he could know that, in less than a decade, Colonel Ourumov would rise from the dead to become a thorn in his side and place him in even greater danger.

3

High Stakes

The south of France, Bond often reflected, was not what it used to be. That coastline which runs from Saint-Tropez to the Italian border, just to the east of Menton, was packed to capacity during the season. The once leisurely Promenade des Anglais in Nice was even more leisurely, but today it was because of the steady, slow-moving stream of traffic – cars and an abundance of tour buses – which made it more like Paris in the late afternoon.

Now, in the early summer of 1995, Bond detested the crowds, the traffic and the obvious growth of pollution, not only in the air, but also in the sea itself. There was trouble in what used to be paradise.

At this moment, however, he had risen above it all as he swung the old Aston Martin DB5 into a hairpin bend on the Grand Corniche, the highest of those roads which run parallel to the coast, in the foothills of the Alpes Maritimes. Up on this snake of a road which is perched on the cliff-like outcrop and sometimes even lances through tunnels blasted into the rock itself, you were removed from the snarl of traffic and crowds, yet afforded magnificent views of the sea and coastline.

He had almost forgotten what a joy it was to drive the Aston Martin which handled like the thoroughbred it was. Just as much of a thoroughbred as the beautiful Caroline who sat beside him.

Caroline had not struck him as a girl who frightened easily, but he could feel her nervousness as he accelerated along the straight. When she spoke it was in the cultured accent of a young woman who had been brought up in an atmosphere of relative privilege and had never felt guilty about it.

'James, do we really have to go quite so fast?' She glanced at him and then turned her attention quickly back to the road, for a large truck was rounding the bend taking up more of the Aston Martin's road than it should.

Bond shifted down to third, and eased the car over so that the two vehicles passed safely with around an inch between them.

'Speed, my dear Caroline, is one of the few true aphrodisiacs left to mankind.' He gave her a wicked smile, the cruel mouth lifting in pleasure while his startlingly ice blue eyes twinkled.

Caroline swallowed. 'I prefer soft lights, music and champagne,' she said bluntly.

'That's good as well.'

'James, I like a spirited drive as well as the next girl, but. . . .'

'Well, what've we got here?' His head turned as a bright yellow Ferrari 355 pulled alongside, its driver glancing across with a mocking smile.

The driver had a dark gypsy look about her, and the smile held a hint of challenge that Bond could not ignore as the Ferrari eased ahead of him.

'Who the blazes is that?' Caroline's hand came up, touching Bond's arm for a second. It could have been the start of a proprietary gesture, but she pulled the hand back, asking the question again.

'Haven't a clue.' Bond did not even look at her. 'But from here she has good lines, and she's certainly shaking her tail at us.' He gently accelerated, bringing the car to within a few feet of the Ferrari, following her exact line as she increased speed on another sharp bend, forcing Bond to shift down and tap the brakes, losing a little distance, which he made up quickly on the straight stretch of road ahead. This time he pulled out, piled on the power and shot past the Italian car.

'James, stop this. You're. . . .'

'Flirting with death?' He tapped the brakes again as they came to another long treacherous bend.

'You're flirting with something,' she began, then gasped as the Ferrari shot ahead, its driver not even turning her head, her eyes totally concentrating on the road.

Bond shifted down, floored the accelerator and then shifted up, now close behind the Ferrari. The girl driving the car in front swung out, in a desperate attempt to block the Aston Martin, but Bond, seeing his chance, pulled out and roared past, the edge of the road to his left barely a foot away from a long drop over the rocks.

'James, I said stop this,' Caroline's voice cracked with a note of command.

'Only a bit of fun. Where else could you get this kind of thrill, mixed with beautiful scenery and gorgeous weather?'

'James. I was sent out here to do your five-year evaluation. Do you want my report to M . . .' She cut off with an intake of breath as the Ferrari came alongside in an attempt to pass, but Bond was blocking her off, matching

25

speed for speed as the two cars hurtled towards a long right hand bend.

He saw the flashing lights and heard the honking horn of the tour bus a fraction of a second before the Ferrari's driver. For what seemed like a moment suspended in time, the big bus loomed huge in the Ferrari's path.

Bond mouthed an expletive, pumping the brakes and shifting down, slowing the Aston Martin safely and just allowing the Ferrari to cross his nose with only a whisper between the car and the bus. 'Ladies first.' He tried to make it sound amusing, failing miserably.

'Stop this car!' Caroline snapped. 'I mean it, James. Stop this car at once!'

'Whatever you say, Ma'am.' The car slewed straight across the road, burning rubber as it came to a halt sideways on at a tourist overlook. 'No problem, Caroline. I have no problem with female authority, and I hope you'll put that in my evaluation.' His hand moved to the console, one finger flicking a switch. Noiselessly a section below the dash slid back to reveal a chilling bottle of champagne and two glasses. 'I usually keep a gun in there.' He smiled into her light brown eyes. 'But, as this is rather special. . . .'

'What on earth am I going to do with you, James?'

'Drink to my evaluation.' He had filled the two glasses, toasted her and took a sip from his, then put it back on the console, leaned forward and whispered, 'Let's make it a really thorough evaluation.'

She gave a sigh, part despair and part desire as she lifted her head to receive his mouth on her own.

In the distance, the principality of Monaco shimmered in the afternoon heat, the harbour lined with several million dollars worth of yachts.

*　　*　　*

He noticed the distinctive yellow Ferrari as soon as he pulled the Aston Martin into the Casino's parking area. He was not even thinking about the race on the Grand Corniche, for Bond's mind was on Caroline. Were those really tears he detected in her eyes as she held him close on saying goodbye at Nice airport?

He hoped that she was not going to be a clinging vine. That was the trouble with some women, even in these days of liberation and equality. You still got clingers now and again, and one like Caroline would be awkward because she obviously had the ear of the recently appointed M. As far as Bond was concerned, the new M was not the greatest news of the year – even though the media had made a huge fuss. Bond was not a great fan of the media either, particularly now that the Secret Intelligence Service appeared to have ditched the word secret.

Then he saw the Ferrari and thought the night's gambling might just be made a shade more amusing.

At the entrance to the *Salles Privées* the blue jowled and immaculate duty manager acknowledged Bond by name, suggesting that the real action this evening was at the *banque à tout va* – the baccarat table. Certainly there was a small knot of people watching the game, and Bond saw that the centre of attention was the attractive dark-haired young woman who had cheated death with him on the Grand Corniche that afternoon.

She wore a simple black dress and a diamond choker at her neck. The diamonds could well be real, and she certainly looked like the proverbial million dollars. As she glanced up, he saw that the gypsy look he had caught from the glimpses of her in the car came from the jet black eyes and the smoothness of her hair which had a depth of texture to it that reminded him of a bolt of sheer silk. High cheek bones, a strong nose and a wide mouth made her very desirable.

She had just won, for he heard the croupier call out '*Sept à la banque.*' He slid a very large number of plaques and chips across to the woman who indicated that she wanted them added to her considerable pile already on the table.

The little Japanese man sitting next to her shook his head and in good, very audible, English said that this was too rich for him. The croupier swept around the players to find someone to bet against her. Four men and one other woman who had obviously been playing, refused – which was not surprising as there must have been well over £100,000 on the table.

At the last moment Bond softly said, '*Banco.*' Coming out from behind the crowd, he took an empty chair facing her and matched the large bet.

The girl acknowledged his nod and slipped two cards from the *sabot* – as the croupiers thought of what mere mortals always called the shoe – dealing them towards him.

He picked them up and glanced at them. Not brilliant: a red two and a black five. Looking across at her he smiled. 'It seems that we share the same passions. Well, three of them anyway . . .' shaking his head to refuse a third card.

Her voice was soft with a slight accent which made him frown as he tried to place it.

'I count two passions only. Motoring and baccarat.'

He gestured, showing no surprise as she turned over her cards – an ace and a seven. A natural eight.

'*Huite à la banque,*' intoned the croupier, and Bond felt the tension in the cluster of people who watched the game. Baccarat, he thought, was about the only card game where

28

no skill was needed, and fortunes were won or lost on the turn of a card.

Bond tossed his cards onto the table and watched as the croupier scooped up his bet.

'I hope your third is where your real talent lies.' Her voice mocked him.

'Oh, I hope I can rise to any challenge.' His smile had turned cynical and the croupier started to push his plaques and chips towards the young woman.

She shook her head. 'Double.'

'*Suivi.*' Bond redoubled the enormous bet and the croupier looked towards the head croupier sitting on the high chair behind him. Even he glanced towards the duty manager who gave a scarcely perceptible nod to indicate that his credit was good.

The woman's smile turned to one of interest. He could see the thought deep in her black eyes – is this man for real or is he just a fool? She nodded and dealt the cards.

Glancing at his cards, Bond asked for a third – '*Carte.*'

She looked at him for a long moment, trying to make a decision. Then she turned over her cards. A five and a queen, as she dealt Bond a face up six.

'*Cinq,*' the croupier snapped, and Bond turned up two pictures: a king and a jack.

'Six.' The croupier switched to English – 'The bank loses,' as he gathered up the pile of markers and slid them towards Bond.

The woman gave a small shrug, as though losing was an occupational hazard. She rose to leave the table, once more nodding towards Bond. 'Enjoy it while it lasts.'

'It's the way to live life. Enjoy everything.' This time his meaning was quite plain. *Why not enjoy some of it with me?* She did not look back as she walked away.

Her stride reminded him of a cat – a soft and purposeful unhurried tread.

Bond took two of the larger plaques, denoting high figures in French francs, and tossed them to the croupier, as is the custom. He also indicated that he wanted the head croupier to see to his winnings, then he sauntered out into that area of the casino which used to be called the Kitchen – because the games were strictly downmarket money – and is now a pleasant bar area.

He caught up with the woman as she headed towards an empty table.

'And is that the way you live life? Enjoying every moment?' he asked.

She turned to see who had spoken, and there was the hint of a frown on her face. 'Ah, yes. But I usually manage to leave while I'm ahead.'

'So do I, but I've never completely mastered the trick.' He signalled to a passing waiter. 'A vodka martini for me. Shaken not stirred, and for you?'

'Oh, the same. I prefer the vodka, though the experts say this is not correct.'

'Experts are not always correct.'

The waiter acknowledged the order, asking her how she would like her martini.

'Straight up, with a twist.' Then, as the waiter moved away. 'Thank you, Mr . . . ?'

'The name's Bond. James Bond.'

She reached across the table and shook his hand. 'Xenia Onatopp.'

'Onatopp?'

'Onatopp.' She nodded.

'And the accent. Do I detect . . . Georgian?'

'Very good, Mr Bond. You're a veritable Professor Higgins.'

In the back of his mind an alarm went off, for the accent was pure Muscovite. She had learned her English in Moscow where she had been born and bred. Learned it at school or, more likely, from the old KGB.

She was silent until the waiter served their drinks. Then, 'You have been to Russia, Mr Bond?'

'Not for a while. But I used to visit. Usually flying visits.'

'It's a very different country now. Truly a land of opportunity.'

'Yes, I'd heard. With a new Ferrari in every garage.'

She gave a little laugh. It was meant to be bell-like, but the bell was cracked. 'The Ferrari. That belongs to a friend.'

'Then let me give your friend a tip. The French registration plates for this year's model start with the letter L. Even the counterfeit ones.'

Deep within her black eyes, he thought that he detected a flinch, but she recovered quickly. 'And what rank do you hold with the motor vehicles department, Mr Bond?'

'Commander.'

'Ah.' She was looking at a point just over his left shoulder. Smiling at someone. He turned his head and saw a tall, distinguished-looking man approaching them. He wore the dress uniform of an admiral of the United States' Navy, and had the leathery, tanned and windblown face which women find attractive. While he carried himself in that instantly recognisable style of a man more used to pacing the bridge of a ship, there was also something rakish about him. Perhaps it was the flecks of grey at his temples, or possibly the well-trimmed beard. It was certainly not a sense of humour, for his eyes had that smoky dead look that comes from spending a great deal of time staring towards a far horizon.

'You ready, Xenia?' He completely ignored Bond.

Xenia smiled sweetly. 'This one's an admiral. Admiral Farrel, Commander Bond.'

He had a firm handshake, but did not quite look Bond in the eye. 'Chuck Farrel, US Navy.'

'James Bond, Royal Navy.'

Xenia rose and linked her arm through the admiral's.

'I respect a woman who can pull rank on me.' Bond did not smile.

'It's been nice meeting you, Commander Bond.'

'My pleasure.'

As they headed towards the exit, so the duty manager came over with a cashier's cheque for Bond's winnings. 'You were lucky tonight, Mr Bond. Pity about the lady.'

'Yes, isn't it?' His mind was not really on the reply for he was waiting just long enough to let Xenia and her pet admiral get clear. There was definitely something wrong about the woman. It was time, he considered, for him to get in touch with London. In fact it was essential, urgent, for he had a nasty feeling that lives could be at stake.

4

The Spider and the Admiral

A small square stands directly in front of the Renaissance royal palace, high on the rock above Monaco. The cathedral is only a few yards away, and alleyways lead off the square. Some of the unsung but excellent eating places in the principality can be found in these small streets, while the square itself is a popular haunt of tourists.

Usually the instamatic, Doctor Scholl-sandled tourists gather in the square to watch the changing of the guard which has a light operetta, toy soldierish air to it.

The sentry boxes are painted in white and red, and the guards themselves could have stepped straight from the pages of some Ruritanian novel. Most visitors think it charming. Older residents regard the tourists as vulgar folk who have come from another planet.

On the Mediterranean side of the square, old and defunct cannon point helplessly out to sea. On the opposite side there is a clear view of the harbour and yacht basin of Monte Carlo.

On this warm velvet night, a tourist group watched a mime performing in the square, while others gazed out at the twinkling, floodlit harbour. James Bond did more than gaze. He stood looking down on the harbour, feet planted apart as though he stood on the bridge of a warship, a large pair of night glasses glued to his eyes.

These were far from ordinary night glasses, but another product of Q Branch's fertile imagination. Not only was the image quality enhanced to a point where, at this moment, he could have been standing next to the couple in his sights, but also the binoculars contained the ability to photograph the exact scene onto which he was zeroed – the resulting pictures stored immediately on a small computer disk within the centre section of the glasses.

Down among the berthed yachts, he had two people in close up. The slim and dark Xenia Onatopp and her admiral who, to Bond, looked incredibly like the long ago murdered Czar Nicholas.

Admiral Farrel was handing the delicious and mysterious Xenia into a motor launch. Bond pressed the camera button twice – once for the admiral and once, full face, for Onatopp, then a third time for the insurance. He moved slightly to focus in on the stern of the launch, magnifying the name *Manticore*.

The launch, leaving a white trail of foam behind it, sped from the jetty, heading out towards a sleek and very expensive yacht at anchor in the harbour.

Bond waited a few minutes, examining the other ships visible inshore and in the harbour. Among them he noticed the lines of a French warship. This last had a long stern which was almost completely taken up by a large helicopter. In silhouette the machine looked dark and full of menace.

Something in the back of Bond's mind stirred, half surfaced then again retreated from his memory. He pushed it away. If you cannot recall something immediately, it probably is not worth remembering anyway. Meanwhile he had things to do.

The walk down from the rock took him some ten minutes, so within a quarter of an hour he was behind the wheel of the DB5, growling out of Monaco again and heading high up into the foothills. Eventually he parked just below the ancient village of La Turbie, with its Roman ruins and monument. It was the place, they had told him, where he would get the best possible reception.

Turning on the radio, he quickly unloaded the little computer disk from the binoculars, slid it into a slit to the right of the CD player and pressed one of the preset radio buttons. There was an almost imperceptible whine as the data was read from the disk and carried to London via satellite.

It took ten minutes, almost to the second. The radio crackled and he heard the voice of Moneypenny who, in spite of her long association with the old M, had agreed to see the recently appointed Chief through the first difficult months in charge.

'Transmission begins.' Bond smiled as her slightly breathy voice came clearly into the car through its eight speakers, and at the same moment a fax began to emerge in full colour from the CD slot.

The first photograph was of Xenia. Moneypenny kept up her running commentary. 'ID confirmed. Onatopp, Xenia. Former Soviet fighter pilot. Worked for a year, just before the '91 coup, as a general pilot for KGB. Current suspected link with the St Petersburg Janus Crime syndicate.'

Next came his shot of Chuck Farrel. 'ID confirmed. Rear Admiral Charles (Chuck) Farrel, US Navy. Distinguished career as an expert in the use of naval helicopters. Career marred only by rumours of constant womanising.

Was cleared of several charges during the now infamous *Tailhook* scandal in 1993. Is in Monaco with a number of US Navy personnel gathering for a top secret demonstration.'

Last came the name *Manticore* on the rear of the motor launch.

'Yacht, *Manticore*, is on lease to a known Janus corporation front. M authorises you to observe subject Onatopp, but not – repeat not – to make contact without M's personal authority. End transmission.'

She had stressed the word 'contact' as though it were a code word for something more interesting. The Janus Crime syndicate was, he knew, the most ruthless of the organised Russian mafia families that had become more deadly than anything conceived during the last days of the Soviet Union. Janus was the scourge of the new Russia and one of the reasons why Bond held to the theory that, eventually, it would be business as usual within the shrinking borders of the once evil empire.

It was time, he thought, to pay a visit to this yacht, *Manticore*, something that was easier said than done.

The main stateroom of *Manticore* was overtly designed for physical pleasure. It was a relatively larger cabin with an en suite bathroom big enough to sport a Jacuzzi and wall fittings that contained colourful bottles full of brand name oils and unguents, including those sensual edible oils sold as sexual aids – the ones that come in various flavours which enable partners to lick them from each other's bodies.

The walls were decorated with erotic paintings and drawings, culminating with a huge oil directly over the bed depicting in all its detail a modern view of a Roman orgy. The lights were dimmed and there was a scent of musk in the air, while from some hidden source came a soft lush melody played on what sounded like a thousand strings.

On the bed itself, late on this warm and luxurious evening, Xenia Onatopp coupled with Admiral Chuck Farrel who was slowly understanding that he had never had it so good. She had taken control almost before locking the door to the stateroom and telling him that nobody would disturb them.

She had stripped him, pushed him back onto the great bed and said – 'For this one night, Chuck, I want you to enjoy me fully. Think of me as the ultimate pinnacle of your sexual dreams.'

She had slowly undressed for him, gently revealing her body, not in the vulgar grind of a striptease artist, but with the flair and professionalism of a ballerina. Each movement seemed to have been choreographed just for him, and at last when she was totally naked she came to him, whispering in his ear, rousing him almost to a frenzy, helping him, instructing him as a perfect body slave until he became pliable, and left with a sense that he owed her a great sexual experience.

It was then that she began a true domination of him: straddling his body and riding him, goading him onwards until their sweat mingled and he was completely at her mercy.

He cried out as he reached his summit for the third time in two hours, and, as he did so, she made a quick subtle movement with her thighs, flipping him over so that he lay face downwards on the bed.

With soft, soothing words she began to wrap her strong legs around his body, moving slightly so that eventually she held him in a scissors grip, her thighs wrapped around his chest, slowly loosening and tightening her hold in a manner which made him gasp with pleasure until she suddenly began tensing the muscles as though she were attempting to draw his entire body into hers.

He gasped and cried out – 'Xenia . . . No. I can't breathe . . . I . . . No. . . .'

It was doubtful if she even heard him as she flexed the muscles even tighter. This was the technique of a boa constrictor and she felt the bones crack in his chest, with half her mind registering the inevitable crunching horror of ribs crumbling.

At the moment of his asphyxiation, Xenia Onatopp cried out in her own final and conclusive orgasm – 'Yes . . . Ahhhhh . . . Yes! Yes! . . . Yeeeessssss!'

It was a technique she had used many times during her life, and her masters knew how effective she could be. A secret weapon like a spider who consumes its mate after the sex act.

She swayed to and fro, still rubbing herself against his corpse, moaning and supremely satisfied in her moment of glory.

She flicked the dead body onto its back, then slowly unwound herself, as though woken from a trance by the soft knock on the stateroom door.

She opened up, unconcerned about her nakedness.

A familiar figure stood in the doorway. 'The spider and the admiral, huh?' the man said as he gently took her in his arms and rocked her as one will lull a child into comfort or sleep.

Bond had already taken the small sailing boat along the coastline. Two days before, when M's representative, Caroline, had demanded that he should show her his proficiency with the little craft which he had rented together with the tiny villa, right on the shoreline near Cap Ferrat.

In the early hours of that morning, he prepared for another journey: showering first with scalding water and then with an ice cold needle spray.

He towelled himself down roughly, and went through his exercises, the sit-ups and push-ups that were his normal routine first thing in the morning. The fact that he had been awake all night made no difference for tomorrow was now, and it helped his discipline to act as though he had just risen from a deep and long sleep. He had, in fact, taken a cat nap lasting for less than an hour. Over the years he had learned the art of sleeping, even on his feet, for an accurate amount of time: drawing from this a new energy as though he had taken a full eight hours of refreshment.

He shaved and dressed – slacks, a white sea island cotton shirt, soft espadrilles and blazer – in his usual time, then went through the small living room into the tiny kitchen where he carefully cooked his normal breakfast, or near enough his normal breakfast – the best meal of the day, and the most important he always considered.

The coffee was not his much beloved De Bry brewed in an American Chemex, but it was near enough and brewed in an earthenware jug. He *had* managed to lay his hands on Cooper's Vintage Marmalade, wholewheat bread for his toast and eggs very similar to the ones from French Marans hens. Unhappily there was none of the deep yellow Jersey butter, but he found the local variety very much to his taste.

He took his time over the two cups of coffee, the egg boiled for exactly three and one third minutes and his slices of toast.

He sat for a full hour after eating. It was now almost four o'clock in the morning and the day ahead promised some action, though that niggling little worry remained hidden at the back of his head. He had returned to it time and again during the night, but it remained as elusive as a four-leafed clover.

Before leaving the villa he packed and readied himself for a fast getaway, for he was reasonably certain that, whatever lay in store for him today, M was likely to summon him back to London before long.

Eventually he went down to the short wooden jetty and made ready to cast off. He wanted his timing to be as accurate as possible for he planned to hide in plain sight among the other yachts and small craft which usually dotted the waters around Monte Carlo from first light. Joining the pleasure seekers and lotus eaters of the area, he would simply be one small craft among many.

It was after five in the morning when he finally cast off and set a course out to sea, for he wanted to sail in a wide circle, coming inshore only at the last moment.

The trip was uneventful, and, as expected, he found himself in the company of yachts, sail boats and motor launches by around nine-thirty. *Manticore* rode at anchor in the same position as she had done during the previous evening so he circled the long sleek seagoing yacht at a distance, his eyes raking the ship for signs of life. By nine forty-five he saw the tender being readied on the starboard side – the side nearest the harbour exit to the sea. He also noted that *Manticore* had a second small motorboat, in the water, riding off the stern.

Gently he manoeuvred his craft around to the port side, bringing her close in to the yacht which had a line draped over the side amidships, presumably to be ready should the tender or motorboat decide to come inboard on the port side.

He grabbed at the line and took the strain. It was firmly secured on the deck and strong enough for him to climb with no difficulty, so he tied up his own little sailboat and heaved himself up the curving flank of *Manticore*, nimbly vaulting over the rail, stopping still and silent the moment his feet touched the deck.

He could hear the sounds of orders being issued, and the grumble of the tender's engines from the starboard side. Whoever crewed the vessel was well occupied over there so he slipped for'ard, heading towards the main saloon.

Inside, the saloon was decorated with style and its fittings and furniture were there for comfort – a long bar taking up the length of one side, deep leather armchairs scattered around the entire room which stretched the width of the ship. Paintings of obvious value were set under lights on the walls, and there was a wide passageway running from the saloon for'ard on the port side.

Silently, Bond moved along the passage until he came to an ornate solid carved wooden door. Gently he tried the handle. The door swung open, and he slipped inside, closing it behind him. He was in a bedroom given over to sensuality: a mirrored ceiling, erotica on the walls and the scent of death reaching his nostrils before he saw the shattered body on the bed.

The ports were open, but the incoming breeze did nothing to disperse the odour he had smelled too many times in his life, and there, sprawled hideously on the bed, was the naked and broken body of Rear Admiral Chuck Farrel. In death his face was not in repose. The eyes were fixed on his reflection in the mirror above the bed, his mouth contorted in a wide open grimace as though he had died in some kind of revolting ecstasy.

There seemed to be music drifting into this bizarre scene, and it took a moment for Bond to realise that it was floating in from the French warship he had noted both last night and on his way into the harbour that morning.

He could see the ship dressed overall through one of the ports. He could also see *Manticore*'s tender rapidly crossing the stretch of sea towards the French ship, and in the tender were two people: Xenia Onatopp and the admiral who lay dead in front of his eyes.

The band on the French naval vessel was playing a selection of sea shanties and, as he peered out, he saw the outline of the helicopter. In that moment, the fact for which his mind had been searching since the previous night came into focus. He felt the blood drain from his face and his lips automatically formed one word – '*Tigre!*'

'Of course,' he whispered to himself as all the pieces slotted into place. 'Of course, *Tigre!*' He did not even hear the door open behind him as his brain made several lightning calculations.

5

The Tigre's A Wonderful Thing

There were two of them, dressed like deck hands in striped T-shirts with *Manticore* across the front, black bell-bottomed slacks and soft shoes. As Bond turned, he did not see them as deck hands. He recognised the type. Hoodlums. Trained hoodlums, the kind the bad old KGB used way back then, in their *Boyevaya Gruppa* – their 'combat gangs' that dispensed broken legs and bullets through the backs of heads. One stood three steps inside the stateroom, the other took one pace inside, moving behind, and to his comrade's left.

In the back of his mind Bond baptised them. Tub o' Lard was three steps in, while Big Muscle was behind.

'Come for the body, have you?' As he spoke, Bond feinted to the right, trying to bring Big Muscle forward. It had the desired effect and he came fast as Bond jumped to his left, sticking out his right leg, catching the oncoming man's ankle. Momentum carried Big Muscle forward so that he landed, at speed, head first against the foot of the bed.

By this time, Bond had grappled with Tub o' Lard, a

shorter, heavier, fatter version of the same species as Big Muscle, going close in and grasping with both hands at the man's left wrist, bringing his left knee up hard into the groin so that the thug gave a gurgle of pain and doubled over.

'Makes your eyes water, doesn't it?' He jerked with all his strength on Tub o' Lard's left arm, heard the bone crack out of joint in the shoulder, ducked under the now useless limb, bringing it up to the middle of the man's back, bending him even further forward and hoping to blazes that there were not any more like him within earshot because Tub o' Lard was now screaming with agony, great schoolboy bellows of pain interspersed with Russian oaths.

Bond positioned the man so that his head pointed directly at his partner who had managed to get to his feet, dazed a little, but turning in on Bond as he grappled with the screaming, doubled up, incapacitated assailant. He let go of the wrist, stepped back and brought the hard leading edge of his right hand down in a heavy chop to the back of Tub o' Lard's neck. There was a whoof of pain which seemed to come from deep within his victim who crumpled up and would have collapsed onto the state-room floor if Bond had not caught him by his belt and the neck of his T-shirt, using him as a battering ram, hurling the body head first directly at Big Muscle's face.

The bullet head caught Big Muscle, covering a large amount of territory. The various crunches came, Bond thought, from nose, right cheek-bone and mouth. There was quite a lot of blood. There was also loss of consciousness for both of them.

'You should really try to stay ahead of the game,' he muttered, turning and leaving the stateroom at speed. If this did concern the *Tigre* helicopter sitting on the pad which was the stern of the French vessel, he would have little time to spare.

Manticore was obviously operating with a skeleton crew or some of her crew must be ashore, for there was nobody else on deck. Bond raced to the stern and pulled at the line which reached out to the motorboat he had seen on his way in.

It took time to get the little craft inboard on the starboard side. Time and a lot of sweat, but eventually she was there and he was able to slip down the ladder and jump into the cockpit.

The engine started immediately, at the first try, and he swung the boat away from *Manticore*, pointed it in the direction of the French ship, opened the throttle to full power and, with some relief, felt the craft leap forward and begin to bump across the water.

As he came closer to the warship, he could make out the crowd gathering into a series of raked seats which had been arranged facing the stern and the helicopter. The machine looked like a larger and more chunky version of the old Cheyenne with a big bulbous nose, a long, sleek cockpit canopy and bigger stubby wings from which hung a very mixed bag of weapons – rockets mainly, though above the wing a couple of large calibre machine guns took care of any close-in firing. He should have thought about this sooner: the file had been on his desk before leaving for the evaluation in the field. The *Tigre*, still officially classified, France's advanced piece of flying hardware, was to be shown off to a load of bigwigs whom the French Navy were hosting at an all-expenses-paid junket in Monte Carlo.

When he reached the side of the ship, Bond had to wait in line while two other tenders discharged officers and their wives. In the main they were in uniform and were obviously naval or air attachés or visiting high-ranking diplomats.

Finally, he climbed the ladder and flashed his official card at the young sub-lieutenant. 'Commander Bond. Royal Navy Intelligence,' he snapped as though he would personally rip the nose off anyone who doubted him. The young officer did not even query him as he turned towards the quarterdeck and saluted.

He was walking towards the stern, eyes everywhere looking for Ms Onatopp and her 'Admiral', but they seemed to have disappeared, or were out of view on the port side. On the helicopter pad the *Tigre*'s big engines started up, then were eased back into idle, the main rotor blades turning lazily as a ground crew member climbed down from the high canopy.

He was about to find some way across when there was a familiar click from the public address system and a voice began an official welcome –

'Ladies and gentlemen, we are about to begin the demonstration of this extraordinary aircraft.' The announcement was in French, rapidly repeated in English, German and Italian.

Discreetly, Bond moved through the invited guests and managed to find a seat on the very edge of the viewing platform as the commentary continued –

'What you are going to see is a demonstration of Europe's addition to modern warfare: the first working prototype of the *Tigre* helicopter. Uniquely manoeuvrable, the *Tigre* helicopter not only uses the latest in Stealth technology, but also it is the only helicopter to be hardened against all forms of electronic interference, radio jamming and electromagnetic radiation. Now, the *Tigre*'s test crew are ready. Let me introduce you to Lieutenant-Commander Bernard Jaubert and Lieutenant François Brouse.'

The band struck up 'Those Magnificent Men in their Flying Machines', and two figures appeared from the crew room which was obviously situated somewhere to their right on the port side.

They were already in flight coveralls, with helmets in place, and when they came into Bond's line of vision as they reached the helicopter, he felt a lurch of recognition. The pilot was slightly built, but he could identify the walk anywhere: the cat-like tread of Xenia Onatopp.

There was a pause of maybe three seconds as the two figures swarmed up the ladder taking them to the long domed canopy. They were about to settle into the cockpit and electronics station when Bond leaped to his feet and lunged forward, heading straight towards the helicopter.

There were a couple of screams and some shouts. Bandsmen were scattered, and he had almost reached the edge of the pad before several brawny Naval Police grabbed him.

'Stop them!' he yelled. 'They're not your crew! Stop . . . !' He was thrown to the deck struggling, while the police held him down. He sucked in air and began to shout again, but was drowned out by the *Tigre*'s engines. An officer had joined them and was mouthing something at him, but his hearing was blanked off by the thunder from the chopper.

He threw one of his captors off and battled his way to his feet, still restrained by the other three as he watched the machine take off, lifting very fast and then going into an almost impossible Rate Five turn, something you did not see helicopters do as a rule. There was a scatter of applause from the assembled dignitaries as the helicopter pointed its nose towards the sky and climbed with a speed that seemed to match some jet fighters, then it fell away, doing a perfect Immelman Turn, and at that moment a white-faced naval policeman came running up, almost babbling at the officer – 'They're dead.' He was breathless. 'In the crew room, sir. The flight crew're dead. The Lieutenant Commander's been shot. Lieutenant Brouse has had his throat cut!'

The officer looked around him, as though he were searching for some way to reverse the facts he was hearing. In the distance the engine noise of the *Tigre* was getting fainter.

'You are part of some plot.' He stubbed a finger into Bond's chest. 'Who are you?'

'Commander Bond, Royal Navy. Intelligence. I was trying to warn you.'

'But who the hell . . . ?'

'Janus,' Bond mouthed, his eyes hard and his face set as though carved in hard stone. 'The Russian Janus Crime Syndicate.'

'So, the Janus Crime Syndicate?' M raised an eyebrow and looked across her desk at Bond.

M's office had changed beyond belief since Bond's old Chief had retired. There was no rich smell of his pipe, no soft leather chairs, no hint of the Old Man's brilliant career in the Royal Navy. The new M had brought with her the sterility of the current technocracy. The furniture was almost a parody of high tech office fittings. There was a Scandinavian influence: posture improving chairs, her own chair which was not a chair but something into which you appeared to contort your body.

The black desk held no clutter but for the very large computer monitor and a moveable lamp plus, naturally, several colour coded telephones. M glanced up at Bond and fixed him with a long serious look. She wore a severe black business suit, her hair was styled very short, almost a thin cap on her scalp, at her neck was one piece of jewellery: a single white on blue cameo brooch, clasped high on her blouse.

Looking at her eyes, Bond thought of the old joke about the bank manager with one glass eye. People could always tell which was the glass one because it was the eye that showed compassion.

'So, you say Janus?' She was all business, even brusque.

'I think it follows, ma'am. A known Janus confidante, Ms Onatopp; a yacht belonging to a known Janus front. A disappearing American admiral. . . .'

'Who you say is dead.'

'I saw the body. He was very dead.'

'It's a shade too pat for my liking.'

'You mean Janus is a little ham-fisted, leaving their pawmarks all over the place?'

'Precisely. The yacht had long gone before any authorities could get near. Gone, Bond. Vanished, Bond, as though it had never been. . . .'

'But there is a harbour record that it was there. The criminal organisations of the new Russia are not known for their subtlety, Ma'am.'

She looked up at him to see if he was being frivolous, but his face did not betray his thoughts. The woman could take nothing at face value. He found her constantly querying undeniable facts. Perhaps this was her background, for she was an analyst at heart; a wrangler; a detector of deceit through columns of figures. Since she had taken over, almost everyone within the Service spoke of her as the Evil Queen of Numbers and many said she should really have been assigned to the Inland Revenue Service's Special Office. Within two days of her appointment,

Bill Tanner – the old M's faithful Chief of Staff – had almost resigned when his title was changed to Senior Analyst.

'Yes, indeed, the *Tigre is* a wonderful thing; and it also vanished from the face of the earth. Any ideas on *that*, Commander Bond?'

'That's its function in life, Ma'am. The *Tigre*'s entire purpose is to be invisible. . . .'

'Yes, but. . . .'

'But half the French airforce were scrambled, every tracking station was put on alert? Yes, about twenty minutes after it was stolen. I have my theory on how that little trick was accomplished.'

'How?'

'With what that thing carries, it can remain invisible, except to the naked eye, for up to twenty-four hours. I think the thieves simply put the chopper down in some deserted area – not difficult in the Alps – and camouflaged it, waiting until nightfall and for the search to go cold. Then they simply took off again and did the trip in easy stages.'

M thought about this for some time, her brow wrinkled, fingers drumming on the desk. 'We've done all we can to track the thing. Every last piece of electronic listening and satellite surveillance has the profile. It can't hide for ever.'

Bond wanted to say something like, 'You want to bet?' but controlled his urge as she nodded – a gesture of terse dismissal.

He was almost at the door when a sudden buzz on M's intercom slowed him down.

'They've found the helicopter, the *Tigre*.' Moneypenny sounded breathless. 'They would like you to come down to the Operations Room as soon as possible. Mr Tanner says it is somewhat urgent.'

'You go ahead, 007.' M had already begun to busy her-self at the desk. 'I'll be down shortly.'

'Typical,' he thought, but acknowledged the instruction calmly. 'Where have they found the damned thing?' he asked himself. His intuition told him that the Operations Room had unpleasant news in store, but he had no idea of how serious the situation would really turn out to be.

6

Petya

Some fifty miles inland from the furthest tip of northern Russia where the land spits out into the Arctic Ocean, there is a ruin that was once Severnaya Station, an operational control post for some of the Soviet Union's most terrifying weapons of mass destruction. The ground around the area is for the most part flat, and usually strewn with ice and snow for most of the year.

About half-an-hour before Bond was summoned to the Operations Room at the headquarters of the Secret Intelligence Service in London, a sled, drawn by four dogs, bounced and rolled its way towards the little parcel of ruined buildings. The man who stood at the back of the sled was a *Yuit* Eskimo, and he came from the small settlement close to what had once been a whole village, some two miles from Severnaya Station.

After the people had come to build the now ruined station, many of the *Yuit* had died from diseases brought by the strangers. Only the hardy ones remained, now four families were left in the settlement. They merely wanted to live as their people had always lived, so they had made themselves useful to the strangers just as he was doing by travelling to the nearest township and collecting artifacts which he could sell when the troglodytes came up from under the ground, which they did every six months or so.

The *Yuit* was very tired: anxious to see his family again for the entire trip had taken the best part of a week. Though he would never know it, the accident occurred because of his fatigue and the pace at which he ran the dogs. He did not even see the boulder peeping from the slick ground. The lead dog saw the danger a fraction too late, swerved to avoid the obstacle and swung the sled into an impossible turn. The runners hit the boulder off centre and the driver was thrown hard against a cluster of rocks and ice.

Even with the layers of fur and the big hood he wore, the man broke several bones including his neck. He tried to move but could not even stir for the pain. He lay there in the snow, with the dogs whining and clustering around him. He made a supreme effort, one last great push through the agony, attempting to get up. This last action killed him and he dropped back onto the ground, a little bundle of fur.

The dogs gathered around him for a while, as though trying to give their master some warmth to revive him. After ten minutes or so they sat down and waited. Eventually the lead dog would guide them back to the tiny settlement, but for the moment they kept a vigil over their dead master. Nobody could know how this accident and the unsupervised dog team would save another life in the next few hours.

It was quite soon after the sled accident that the *Tigre* helicopter arrived, bearing its two uninvited guests.

Both British and American analysts had shown an interest in the seemingly defunct Severnaya Station. From the big satellites they had many pictures of the area which the Russians claimed had been taken off the operational list for the past two years. The pictures showed ruin and decay, except for one thing – the huge radio telescope dish that appeared to grow from the ground. The dish had been there for some years, but the pictures seemed to show that it occasionally changed. The analysts maintained that over a very short period of time the dish had become larger and that it moved now and then. There were sceptics, of course, some of them with a great deal of experience and knowledge. The latter pointed out that the dish might well move with the wind, and the idea that it had become larger was an optical illusion caused by changes in the weather, and different angles of the sun.

In fact the dish was larger, and it did move at the command of men and women hidden deep in the earth, some thirty feet below the surface, for the Severnaya Station was far from dormant.

The dish, at this very moment, was locked onto a forgotten piece of former Soviet space junk – in reality a fully operational satellite – over the Middle East. It was being controlled by a young woman sitting at a work-station in a well-lit, windowless, scrupulously clean, spacious computer room.

There were roughly a dozen such men and women, all working in this section of the complex. Not one of them was over forty years of age and they had been chosen from a list of hundreds of potential computer scientists throughout the Federation of Russian States.

Doors to kitchens, rest rooms, dining and sleeping facilities led off from this technical area, and a thick glass wall divided the scientists from a control room, manned by several men and women in uniform. This second section contained a long console replete with digital electronic instruments and switches topped by a vast screen, blank at this moment. Sunk into the wall behind this complex control area, was a brilliant red safe. Next to the safe in scarlet lettering was a notice in Russian which said *Locked. Authorisation Code Required*, and as an extra precaution, a steel electronic gate secured by steel plates directly in front of the safe.

Out among the lines of computers, the girl manipulating the satellite was tall, slender and dark with high cheek bones and clear brown eyes. What marked this girl, Natalya Simonova, from the other technicians was her neatness and the clothes she wore – a long black skirt and a white shirt covered by a patterned waistcoat. Many of her colleagues wore the untidy, shapeless grunge look, or worse. The man to her right was clad in dirty jeans, a *Wired* magazine T-shirt and a black leather motorbike jacket. His hair looked as though it had seen neither shampoo nor comb in a week and his attitude was one of an edgy, spaced-out cyberpunk. Boris Grishenko was indeed all of these things and tolerated by those who controlled the establishment because he was undoubtedly the most brilliant scientist in the entire complex.

Natalya spoke quietly into the small mike attached to a headset –

'Rotate right sixty degrees, ascend to one hundred kilometres.'

The blinking satellite symbol on her monitor moved at her bidding. She smiled as though she had just taught a clever trick to a pet. Her delight was interrupted by a maniacal scream of laughter from Boris. 'I've done it. Done it. . . .'

Natalya glanced at her friend, Anna, who was seated at the terminal on her left. Anna rolled her eyes and made

56

a gesture with her hand which meant to show that he was unhinged.

'Natalya, come and see what I've done.' He had gone into hyper crazy mode, so she walked over and looked at his set-up. Boris, being Boris, had several screens set up in front of him. 'I'm in!' he laughed, a tuneless cackle.

On one screen she saw the Seal of the US Department of Justice.

'Christ, Boris, you've hacked into the US Department of Justice? Do you know what will happen if they trace it? If they trace it to here?'

'Sure, the Chief of Computers'll call me a genius, move me back to Moscow and give me a million bucks – which is never going to happen. . . .'

'They pay us in good hard currency anyway, and to hear you talk sometimes that's what you get – a million.'

'Ach, we all get the same. I'd like a chance to spend it sometime instead of being here, living like a ground hog. . . .'

'A worm more likely.'

'Anyway, the Americans are too stupid to catch me. They can't detect viruses on a hard drive, let alone . . . !' His computer gave a warning beep and the seal dissolved, leaving a message flashing on the screen – UNAUTHOR-ISED ENTRY DETECTED.

'You were saying?' Natalya laughed.

Boris cursed and quickly typed in a command to load a programme of his own. The programme flashed a reminder on his screen – TO SEND SPIKE PRESS ENTER.

He hit the *Enter* key and the prompt changed to – SPIKE SENT.

'Good. Spiked them.'

Natalya shook her head. 'Boris, just hang up.'

'No way.' He turned and looked her straight in the eyes. 'I spiked them, you stupid goose. That programme of mine seizes the phone line of anyone trying to trace me. It jams their modem. They can't hang up.'

He typed another command which brought up another message: INITIATE SEARCH – ENTER PASS-WORD.

'Now what?' from Natalya.

'I enter the password.' He typed ten keys. On the screen the letters were not visible, coming up as a line of black circles. 'Bullets,' he explained.

'I know what bullets are, Boris.'

As he tapped *Enter* again so a map of the world came up on the screen and a red line began to trace the telephone line, the names of places ribboning out as it passed through major junctions or satellites. From Severnaya it tracked straight to St Petersburg, across Europe to angle off over the Atlantic to the United States where it crawled quickly to Atlanta, and stopped, leaving a winking red light over the city.

His screen went blank for a second and was suddenly replaced by the words: FBI HEADQUARTERS, COM-PUTER FRAUD DIVISION.

Boris said something obscene and impossible, then banged sharply on his *Enter* key to clear the screen. 'I need a cigarette,' he snapped moodily and sounding sullen.

'Well, I need coffee.' Natalya glanced at her screen to make sure all was in order and walked towards one of the doors that led to a kitchen.

Boris Ivanovich Grishenko swaggered away from his terminal, as if he were walking off the job, heading for one of the utility doors. He went up the steep angle of stone steps that led to the outside world, grinned at a security camera, pushed open the door and stepped into the cold, bleak landscape.

As he did so, a voice echoed from a concealed speaker – 'Comrade Grishenko, you are using an emergency exit. You have been told before, this is illegal. Get back to the technical area as quickly as possible.'

'Come up and stop me.' Boris was obviously always doing this kind of thing, and had little tolerance for authority, knowing he was probably the most essential computer technician they had.

He pulled out a packet of Marlboro cigarettes. He had bought a huge amount on his last leave, paying with the hard currency the technicians earned. Putting a cigarette between his lips, he flicked at the wheel of his lighter. The flame spluttered for a second and was blown out, as if by some sudden strong wind.

Grishenko raised his eyes. The dark shape of a helicopter was descending onto the landing pad some fifty yards away, its rotors stirring the powdered snow into a white tornado.

The *Tigre* has landed, Xenia Onatopp thought grimly. She popped the sleek canopy and undid her safety harness, reaching down to sling an Israeli-made Uzi onto her right shoulder. She already had spare magazines in pouches on her belt.

'Ready, General?' She spoke into her headset, hearing the general's snarl of response – 'Let's get on with it. I've been ready for some time now.'

They were both in uniform, Xenia with the insignia of a colonel, her partner with that of a general. Bond would have recognised the general immediately, for the last time he had seen him General Ourumov had a gun to the head of his old friend Alec Trevelyan.

Boris Grishenko did a swift disappearing act as soon as he spotted the two officers.

Now, Ourumov kept step with Xenia as they marched purposefully along the side of the ruined building, where ice and snow had been cleared from a path which led to the main door, down wide concrete steps, along a corridor to a security door. A guard sprang to attention and saluted, though General Ourumov seemed to hardly notice the man. He knew exactly what he was doing, looking straight into a camera placed almost at eye level and clearly speaking his name – 'General Arkady Grigorovich Ourumov. Head of Space Division.'

There were a series of fast bleeps as the system went through its voice recognition routine, then the steel security door opened and the pair were through into the most sensitive area where the Duty Officer snapped to attention, his second-in-command hastily rising and buttoning his jacket.

'General, if I'd known you were coming. . . .'

Xenia muttered, 'You'd have baked a cake, yes.'

'You'd have been ready for me, I think, Major. This is an unscheduled test of the Severnaya facility. A war simulation. We shall be test firing GoldenEye. Report status.' He looked up and could see that the computer scientists and technicians behind the thick tinted glass were moving, craning from their work-stations to see what was going on. 'Jump, man. Report status,' Ourumov barked at the major.

'Status normal, sir. Two operational satellites: *Petya* and *Mischa*, both in ninety-minute earth orbit at one hundred kilometres.'

'Good. Here's the authorisation code. Hand me the GoldenEye, today's access numbers and the key, please. I am timing you as from now.' He had already thrown a plastic card down on the small counter, now he ostentatiously brought his left arm up and studied his watch.

The major almost fell over himself trying to get things done correctly, punching in the numbers to unlock the metal gate in front of the safe, using the palm print pad to ID himself, them tapping in the safe's code of the day. The lock beeped different tones – like a digital telephone, then clicked open.

Xenia gestured to the other officer and said that he should open the safety door through to the technical area. 'On a wartime basis, Captain, this entire facility must be open in case there is need to evacuate with little warning.' The captain did not argue.

'Today's codes, sir. The electronic firing key and GoldenEye.' The Duty Officer brought the items from the safe: the key, a plastic card, and a small golden disk in the centre of which was an engraved eye.

'Good. Now, make the blind see.'

The major looked down at the disk and removed a piece of golden tape from the centre of the eye, revealing a circle where the pupil would have been.

'You know how the GoldenEye works?'

'Yes, General. When positioned correctly the disk allows a laser beam to lance through its centre, thus initiating the firing mechanism of the satellite.'

'Good. You have done well, Major. I think that will be all we require.' He turned to Xenia. 'Colonel. You take over.'

Xenia almost lazily unslung her Uzi and put two quick bursts in the direction of the two officers. Then she walked unhurriedly to the door leading to the technicians' area and sprayed everything in sight, changing magazines with an almost robot-like perfection.

Bodies were thrown back against equipment or spun violently, showers of sparks and smoke leaped from computer work-stations. The entire business took less than thirty seconds.

In the small kitchen, Natalya Simonova spilled her coffee and looked up, horror in her eyes.

Back in the main control room Xenia bent down and removed a second firing key hanging on a silver chain from around the dead Duty Officer's neck and went over to the long console at which Ourumov had already taken his place, throwing switches and watching the long screen light up high above the instruments.

With great precision Ourumov slid the GoldenEye disk into a slot, not unlike a CD player. He placed the day's code card in front of him and inserted the key into a lock to the right of the point where the golden disk had slid into place. Xenia had already inserted the key taken from the Duty Officer. 'On my count,' he rapped. 'Three, Two, One, Zero.'

They turned their keys in unison and the rest of the console lit up, needles flicked and the screen above them showed a segment of the earth with one of the satellites in orbit.

'Set target acquisition for *Petya*. Severnaya,' the general ordered.

High above the earth's surface, a piece of what appeared to be space junk – possibly the burned out stage of a rocket – seemed to be tumbling around in orbit, but, as the command from Severnaya leaped silently through space to wake it up, so the satellite coded *Petya* emitted blasts from hidden propulsion units and began to change course.

Inside the control room, both Ourumov and Xenia looked at the screen above them and saw what Natalya had been watching, less than half-an-hour before. The red symbol that was the *Petya* began to move rapidly, shifting from its position over the Middle East and heading at an unthinkable speed towards northern Russia.

On a lower display screen information started to ribbon out:

PETYA LOCATION: 80.31.160.17

TARGET: 78.08.107.58.

Then:

TIME TO TARGET: 15.43.21

Ourumov, consulting the card containing the codes, began to punch in a series of numbers. The display now flashed a further message:

WEAPON ARMED.

At that very moment, panic stricken at what she could hear, Natalya knocked over her cup. In the sterile silence the noise was like a hand-grenade exploding.

Both Ourumov and Xenia jerked back.

'Check it,' the general said in a low voice and, as Xenia walked away, so the second-in-command, sprawled in his own blood on the floor, moved. Close to death it was almost a reflex action. His hand shot up and punched one of the many alarm buttons in the room. Xenia whirled around, giving him a quick final burst from the Uzi, but it came a fraction too late, and their ears were assaulted by a sudden shrieking of warning sirens and alarms.

Xenia, pausing, looked anxiously at the general who said, 'Get on with it. Their best response time is seventeen minutes. This place will be hit in less than fifteen now. Go.'

In the kitchen, Natalya pulled a chair to a point directly under the maintenance grille in the room's ceiling, and started to work on loosening the metal. She had pulled it halfway down when she heard the rapid footsteps of Xenia coming hell for leather down the passageway.

Miles away, at the Anadyr air base in Siberia, three MiG-23MDL – 'Flogger-Ks' – hurtled off the main runway. The pilots had only just come on duty when the alarm sounded, and they received the target information literally as they were taxiing from their bunkers. In seconds they would be on their way to Severnaya Station.

Xenia kicked the kitchen door open, saw the broken cup and the spillage of coffee, then looked at the chair and the metal grille above it, now dangling, ripped from its setting.

She smiled grimly and lifted the Uzi spraying the entire ceiling, changing magazines and blasting away again. Nobody hiding up there could possibly live.

Back at the console, she told Ourumov that she had dealt with the matter. He nodded with a tiny smile on his lips, then gestured towards the timers ticking down at what appeared to be a very fast pace.

'Time flies, Colonel.'

'They have a saying in the West.' She grinned at him. 'Time flies, particularly when you're having fun.'

He nodded again, slipped the GoldenEye disk from the console and placed it in his briefcase which he closed with the finality of a coffin lid.

'I think we should get out of here.'

Using the voice print security system again, they left, once more marching in step, up the concrete stairs and out into the cold.

In less than four minutes the *Tigre* helicopter was starting to lift off in a cloud of snow, from which it emerged, black and sinister.

Below the earth, in the small kitchen, one of the cupboard doors squeaked and opened as Natalya crawled out.

In London, James Bond was just entering the Operations Room below the Secret Intelligence Service's headquarters.

7

EMP

Bond went down to the Operations Room with Moneypenny who, he had to admit, was looking more than usually ravishing in a simple black dress with a gold clasp just below her right shoulder.

'Dressed to thrill,' he murmured to himself as they got into the lift.

'I beg your pardon?' She had just caught what he had said. Moneypenny's hearing was almost unnaturally acute. The old M used to say that she could hear the rumours from the powdervine directly from her office.

'I was observing that I've never seen you look so lovely.'

'Well, thank you, James.'

'Got some special assignment on tonight?'

'Well, I don't sit around all the time waiting for you to call. I have a date, if you're really interested. A date with a gentleman. We're going to the theatre.'

'Nothing too taxing, I trust.'

'Shakespeare actually. *Love's Labours Lost.*'

'I'm devastated. What will I ever do without you?'

She gave a coy little smile. 'So far as I recall, James, you've never had me.'

He gave her a sidelong glance. 'No, but it's often been my midsummer night's dream.'

Moneypenny turned her head away. 'James, you know that kind of talk could easily be classed nowadays as sexual harassment.'

'So what's the penalty?'

The lift came to a halt and the doors opened. As she stepped out, Moneypenny tossed a look over her shoulder, eyes twinkling. 'Some day, James, you have to make good on your innuendoes.'

She led the way through to the Operations Room. All the screens were active and the men and women who work below ground for the SIS sat at desks with smaller monitors, or listening through headphones, while senior officers examined maps and spoke quietly to each other.

Bond's closest friend in the world of secrets, Bill Tanner, the old M's faithful Chief of Staff, detached himself from the knot of senior officers and headed for Bond and Moneypenny, his hand stretched out. 'Good to see you again, James.'

'What's going on, Bill? This looks like the old days.' He gestured at the satellite pictures coming in and the large video wall. They all showed similar views – barren, snow-covered land with ruins and the big radio telescope dish.

'It's more than like the old days. This time it looks very unpleasant. About ten minutes ago we intercepted an alarm signal from the supposedly abandoned radar station at Severnaya. . . .'

'Right up north?'

'Just about as far north as you get. Just look at what

our satellite intelligence picked up.' He gave an order to one of the technicians and the picture on the video wall rewound itself, froze screen and then enlarged.

'We've got a match. Your missing *Tigre*.'

There it was, the black shape quite clear against the snow. The technician opened up a smaller screen next to the video screen and up came the helicopter again, shown in both plan and section.

'From Monte Carlo to the far north of Russia. That's quite a leap.'

'Personally, I think that it completes your own theory about the Janus syndicate. Pity the Evil Queen of Numbers won't let you run with the ball.'

'You were saying?' M's voice came from right behind them.

'I was just. . . .'

'Making an unnecessary comment on a nickname I have already heard, Mr Tanner. I happen to believe in numbers. Numbers are more accurate than human beings.'

'With respect, Ma'am, numbers are only as pure and accurate as the person who's inputting them.'

'That goes without saying.' She gave Tanner a look that would cause concern to the toughest of men. 'Now, the Prime Minister's waiting for an update on the situation, so please proceed with your briefing, Mr Tanner.'

Bill Tanner paused for a moment, then walked across to the video wall. Bond had never seen Bill Tanner fazed by anyone, and the new M, hard as she was, seemed to have little effect on him.

'After the distress signal, James, the helicopter took off. Seconds later the Russians scrambled three "Flogger-Ks" from the Anadyr base. They're heading towards Severnaya, as is some unidentified piece of space junk – at least that's what we've always thought it to be.'

'Severnaya's supposed to have been dormant since '90, you think it's operative again?'

'I think it's been operative all the time. The ruins and general mess around it are, I believe, merely cosmetic.'

'So what're they using it for?'

'There was a time,' Tanner looked very troubled as he spoke, 'when we suspected that Severnaya might just be the ground control station for that secret space-based weapons programme they coded GoldenEye. But . . .'

M chipped in. 'But our statistical analysis; our electronic and satellite intelligence could see they had neither the funds nor the technology to implement it.'

'Statistics, Ma'am, were never my strong point. Elint and Satint only go so far. With respect, you can read numbers from these sources, you can analyse them, but you can't get into the heads and hearts of the people operating whatever your target happens to be. These pictures live?'

M gave a short, dismissive laugh. 'Unlike the American government we prefer not to get bad news from CNN. Of course they're live.' She looked up and, like the rest, saw the pulsing red icon, the highlit area of Severnaya, and the moving pinpoints of light that were the Russian aircraft, heading towards the facility.

Below the ground at Severnaya, Natalya stood in the doorway, looking at the ripped and sprawled bodies of her friends. She felt shock and disgust, also a terrible fear seemed to clutch at her, icing her heart and sending her into a momentary depression.

She looked up at the map, saw the counters below it ticking off their numbers, took in the various icons and symbols, knowing what it meant. With that knowledge came action. She turned and dashed for the door that led towards the sleeping quarters. She had to get out of here very quickly indeed, and, if she had to face the snow and ice above ground, she needed more than the black skirt, the shirt and the skimpy underwear she wore with comfort in the air conditioned, underground facility which had been her natural habitat.

In her room she quickly changed into thermal underwear, jeans and her stout leather boots which she had bought during her last leave. She shrugged herself into a thick fur coat, jammed a fur hat onto her head and was already drawing on fur-lined gloves as she ran back to the charnel house that had been the work area . . .

She could not hear the three jets, now in tight formation, at four thousand feet above the complex, their leader talking to base, saying that all seemed normal.

Above the aircraft, things were far from normal. The piece of space junk was changing shape, a hundred kilometres up. It appeared to detach pieces of charred and blackened metal that were merely outer covering. *Petya* was revealing itself as a hard steel core, while around it, a series of shields fanned out, like the ruff which opens up on some threatened reptile. Then, as it rolled slightly downwards, it detonated.

The immediate area around Severnaya was suddenly lit up by a cone-shaped blinding light. Within the light there were hundreds of writhing electrical charges, like long blue snakes.

Two of the 'Flogger-Ks' – one stationed just above the other – were immediately engulfed in coils of electricity. The upper aircraft seemed to be slammed down by the charge. The two aircraft merged together as one in a brilliant flash and explosion.

The lead 'Flogger-K' was hit by a similar bolt of electricity. It simply turned on its back and began to plunge earthwards, the pilot desperately pulling on the eject handle. He was still pulling when the machine bulleted into the huge radio telescope dish and burst into a fireball.

Below ground, Natalya Fyodorova Simonova thought there had been an earthquake. The entire complex shook violently and was plunged into darkness so that she found herself in the middle of the technical area with crackling blue lights circling and in constant movement around the masses of electronics which were scattered across the once pristine, hygienic computer room.

Her fear fed on the already obvious need to escape, and by the flickering deadly lights she dodged across the room, through what had been the main control section, stepping over the Duty Officer's body, then running to the voice recognition unit. Twice she called out her name, but nothing happened. She thought of Boris and again crossed the minefield of ceaseless electrical charges, making her way towards the now blocked utility escape door.

At one point, when she had almost reached the door, Natalya screamed as a great creaking started above her. She leaped to one side as two wall-mounted monitors came hurtling down. Then the creaking began in earnest and she saw in the dim light that the ceiling had begun to cave in.

She had never known dread or claustrophobia like this before. Her years of working in closed off facilities had never once produced anxiety or the horrible vision of being buried alive. Now it had changed. If she had to claw her way out, she would do it. Above her the groaning of weight against stressed concrete became louder; grit began to fill the air, stinging her eyes and drying her throat. She clasped a hand over nose and mouth, and when the final crash came she pushed her back against the wall as though it might be possible to physically penetrate the brick, steel and concrete.

Blood pounded in her ears and the rending, tearing, sliding sound of a whole section of the bunker finally giving way removed, for a moment, all her senses.

With a final grinding explosion half the roof collapsed, and with it the electronics and part of the huge radio telescope dish, mingled with pieces of the aircraft.

It was only when the dust started to clear and she felt the cold night air descending into what could have been her tomb, that Natalya began to move forward. Slowly at first, and then, as some of her courage returned, more surefooted. She climbed and thought of her grandfather's big old apple tree she had climbed as a child. For a few moments she seemed to be fantasising that it was the tree itself, not flat and unstable concrete slabs, that it was summer again and her grandfather was chuckling, calling her a little monkey as she went upwards through the branches and leaves.

Then she remembered Boris, and recalled he was going out for an illegal smoke. She began to call, as she climbed into winter high above her – 'Boris! . . . Boris Ivanovich! . . . Boris, can you hear me?'

She was out in the cold, fresh, clear night air, standing alone in the snow.

Tanner was still standing with M and Bond when the screens went blank with a searing white flash.

'What the bloody hell was that?' Tanner jumped visibly; M flinched, and Bond moved, as though ready to throw himself to one side. Seconds later both M and Tanner had grabbed telephones.

(Far away, Xenia Onatopp and General Ourumov, in

the *Tigre*, felt themselves thrown from side to side as the machine bucked to the snarling rhythms of the dancing snakes of blue electrical fire which reached them, even fifty miles away. Xenia thought to herself that the French had done well. The *Tigre* was indeed invincible.)

Bill Tanner called out from the telephone – 'Our satellite's been knocked out; so have two of the Americans'. We've got one coming into range any second.'

The screens cleared and the satellite images were replaced on the screen. Severnaya dark, except for odd spot fires. Then the dish, tilted and askew, with the wreckage of the burning 'Flogger-K'.

'Good God,' someone said.

'Two of the "Floggers" are down. Power's out. . . .'

M moved closer. 'Looks as though the third aircraft went into the dish.' She turned her head and asked Bond, 'What do you think, 007?'

He had been standing calmly trying to analyse what he could see. 'Well, the buildings are standing. No car or truck movement. Not even a headlamp. I'd say EMP.'

Tanner nodded. 'That would account for the aircraft and satellites. . . .'

'And the cars,' Bond added.

Bill Tanner turned to M. 'EMP, Ma'am. Electro-Magnetic-Pulse. A first strike weapon developed by. . . .'

M cut in, 'I know what EMP is, Mr Tanner. Developed by both the Americans and the Soviets during the Cold War. Someone wrote about the theory after Hiroshima. Set off a nuclear device in the upper atmosphere; this creates a pulse – a radiation surge actually – that destroys anything with an electronic circuit.'

As she paused, so Tanner spoke again, 'The idea was a weapon with which to knock out the enemy's communications before he . . . she . . . they . . . could retaliate.'

M turned to Bond. 'So, is this GoldenEye? Does this mean GoldenEye actually exists?'

'Yes.'

'Is there any chance this could be an accident?'

'Absolutely not, Ma'am, and this would explain the theft of the helicopter. It's the perfect get-away vehicle if you wanted to steal a GoldenEye. You set the thing in motion, so that nobody can stop it. This, in turn, poses a problem. You have to get clear and wipe out all the evidence at the same time. I suspect GoldenEye is a unique triggering and guidance device. If you want to steal it, clean the place of any traces, you get out in something like *Tigre*.'

'So, you think its's your wretched Janus Crime Syndicate?' There was just a trace of bitterness in her voice.

'Not necessarily.' Bond shook his head. 'I've been inside that kind of Russian facility.' He peered at the screens. 'The security is, as the younger generation would say, awesome. Voice-print activators only – which means you can keep the need-to-know down to a bare minimum. You could even keep Yeltsin out of one of these places. You would need two keys to fire the weapons; special access codes kept in a digital wall safe, the access to which is altered daily.' He paused, frowning. 'There had to be an insider for this to work.' He asked one of the technicians to switch to infra-red.

'Now zoom in. No, to your right. A little bit more. There.' The image left a lot to be desired, but a figure was climbing out of the wreckage around the base of the dish.

'As we can all see, someone is climbing out, which means that at least one person probably knows where the leak is; who it is.'

Natalya was in the clear now, but the cold bit even

through the layers of clothes she wore. She made herself go on, dragging one foot after another. The nearest village was at least twenty-five miles, but there was a small railway station twenty miles up the road. Trains were infrequent . . . if she could make it that far.

She heard the dogs whining and barking before she saw them, disoriented and anxious pulling the wooden sled around in circles.

She thanked God, if there was a god. This could be her way out. Maybe she would get to climb that apple tree again some day.

8

Assignment GoldenEye

M was talking on the secure telephone when Bond arrived at her office. Moneypenny – usually keeper of M's inner sanctum – had already gone off duty, but M waved him in, pointing to a chair in front of her desk.

'Sit,' Bond thought. 'Sit. Good dog.' He looked up at the wall behind her desk and wondered what the old M would have thought of the picture hanging there. In his day the old M had managed to get works of art on loan from the Ministry of Works. They were usually scenes of great naval battles or paintings of the sea.

The new painting was of different coloured rectangles, divided by triangles. 'A daub,' the Old Man would have called it. He would have hated it as much as he would have loathed the sterile atmosphere of the new office.

M finally completed her conversation with whoever had been on the other end of the line. The Prime Minister, Bond guessed as M lit a cigarette, inhaled deeply and blew out the smoke in a long thin stream.

'That can damage your health, Ma'am, but I'm sure you know that already.'

She gave him the fish eye but did not answer. Instead she said, 'The Prime Minister's talked with Moscow. They're saying it was an accident during a routine training exercise.'

'No comment on the type of weapon, I presume?' He allowed a thin smile, looking directly at M, as she shook her head. He shrugged, 'Governments change, but the lies stay the same.'

M grunted, and for a moment, Bond thought he was back with the Old Man who used to grunt regularly to avoid commenting on some questions.

'Tell me what else we know about the Janus Crime Syndicate.'

'Very big in the arms trade. Good smugglers with contacts everywhere. Their headquarters are in St Petersburg and they were the first people who managed to get new supplies into Iraq during the Gulf War. Their head man's unreliably described – which means our sources are very uncertain. So far the woman, Onatopp, is our only confirmed contact – among the top people that is.'

M grunted again. 'Would you care for a drink?'

What was this? he wondered. A retreat from alienation? 'Well, thank you. Your predecessor kept a very good cognac. . . .'

'I prefer bourbon.' She got up and crossed to a drinks cabinet. 'Ice?'

'Perish the thought, Ma'am. One should never ruin a good glass of spirits with the abominable ice. Nasty habit.'

'Well, I probably have a lot of habits you wouldn't approve of.' She handed him the drink and returned to her seat behind the desk.

'We pulled the files on anyone who might have access, or authority at the Severnaya Station.' Her eyes flicked up to the computer screen which was angled out of Bond's sight.

'The top name on the list is an old friend of yours.' Leaning forward, she pressed a button on a key pad and the daub of a painting slid from sight, exposing a video monitor. It flickered on and there was Ourumov in full uniform, with data scrolled out beneath.

Almost in a whisper, Bond mouthed silently, 'Ourumov, and they've made him a general.' Aloud, he said, 'A better picture than the one that was there.'

'I agree, that thing is only to left foot people coming into the office for the first time. A simple psychological trick. Someone sits down and the picture is the first thing they look at. I am the second, but I will have had time to take a good look at them.' She gave him a smile that could easily be construed as an exchange of confidences. 'Now, Ourumov. Yes, they've made him a general. More than that, he's a high flyer these days. He sees himself as the next Iron Man of Russia. It's mainly on this count that the analysts've ruled him out. He doesn't fit the profile of a traitor. He's a true son of Mother Russia. You know, the earth and the poppy seeds, all that kind of rubbish.'

'I presume, Ma'am, that these are the same analysts who said that GoldenEye couldn't exist? Who said the helicopter posed no immediate threat, and wasn't worth following?'

She took another sip of her drink and a long pull at the cigarette. 'I was appointed to this job because I'm an analyst, and a good one. I'm also a computer scientist, and have what the PM calls, a razor sharp mind.'

M drew on her cigarette, then stubbed it out. 'I worked for some time under the direct control of my predecessor and *he* assisted in my appointment. The problems are all too obvious. I understand the controls that have been placed upon this Service by the Cabinet, so I understand the way around them.'

She paused again, then looked him straight in the eyes. 'You don't really like me, do you, Bond? You see me as a jumped-up pocket calculator, who's far more interested in my numbers than your own instincts.'

Bond simply nodded assent.

'Well, that's fine by me, because I see you as a sexist misogynist dinosaur. You're a relic of the Cold War.' She smiled. 'It may surprise you to know that I believe very strongly in having people in the field, men and women, who can bore into the hearts and minds of any enemies. I was put here to reorganise and make sure we come in under budget each year, and, by God, I'm going to do that. But to do it properly I know we have to send people out undercover, and some as recruiting agents. That, more than ever before, we need networks, agents working out there at the sharp end. So, if you think, for one moment, that I don't have the balls to send a man out to die in some dodgy foreign field, then your instincts are dead wrong.'

Bond had no reply to this impassioned speech. If anything, he *did* have a tad more respect for the new M, who had started to speak again.

'I have absolutely no compunction about sending you to your death, 007. But I certainly won't do it on a mere whim – even with your cavalier attitude to life and death.'

It was time for him to say something. 'Ma'am, I've never forgotten that a licence to kill is also a certificate to die.'

She gave him a curt nod. 'Good, because I want you to find GoldenEye. I want you to find out who took it – for I'm certain that someone took whatever is necessary to unlock the weapon, just as I'm sure there are more of those things drifting quietly around in orbit. So, you are to find out who stole it and what he, she or it intends to do with it.' She turned and pointed towards the monitor. 'And, 007, if you do happen to run across Ourumov, guilty or not, I don't want you running off on some kind of personal vendetta. Avenging Alec Trevelyan will not bring him back.'

'With respect, Ma'am, you didn't get him killed.'

'Neither did you. Don't make this personal. Understand?'

He paused, pictures of his old friend going through his head. He thought of the training they had been through together, and the operations. For a couple of seconds he felt Trevelyan very close to him, as though he were standing by his shoulder. He saw the ageless face and the cheeky smile. Heard him whisper, 'She's right, James. It just isn't worth it.' Then saw the man's end, with Ourumov pulling the trigger as he knelt on the stone floor of the chemical and biological weapons facility.

'Yes, I understand, Ma'am.' He rose and began to walk towards the door. His hand was on the knob when she spoke again –

'Bond,' she said, her voice a shade softer. 'Come back alive.'

There were two days of intensive briefing, and at the end of all that, he attended a special session, very late at night, with Q. They met in one of the large test and firing ranges deep below headquarters, and Q had only a couple of items for him.

One was an ingenious belt which looked perfectly normal until he pointed out a small catch above the buckle.

'That's the safety,' Q told him. 'Be very careful to keep it in this position at all times – until you need to use it.' He showed him how to take off the safety catch and how to aim the buckle so that, when pressed, the tine – which, in reality, was a neatly designed piton – would shoot out with force, carrying seventy-five feet of high tensile cord. 'That cord is strong enough to support you, James.'

'What if I need extra support?'

Q had smiled grimly. 'Then you'll have to pray. We've only tested it to your weight: but it does work and that little piton will embed itself in practically anything, and hold once it's in.'

The other item was more lethal. What looked like an ordinary pen, but was, in fact, a grenade. Click the top once and you could write with it. Give it three clicks and the four second fuse was armed. Within that four seconds, a further three clicks would disarm the thing.

Q even demonstrated with a dummy which blew apart at the contained explosion from the device.

'The pen is certainly mightier than the sword, 007.' It was the nearest Q ever got to a joke, and Bond looked across at the shattered dummy, remarking that the writing was certainly on the wall.

He looked around to see that Q's working quarters were, as usual, full of strange and exotic pieces of equipment. Eventually, he spotted an ornate silver tray on which there stood a large plate bearing six or seven inches of a French stick, cut in two and filled with tomatoes, onions and tuna.

'What's that?' Bond cocked his head towards the tray.

'Quite interesting really.' Q always became animated when you asked questions about his more complex pieces. 'The tray?' he enquired as though for reassurance.

'The tray, yes.'

'Ah.' Once more a smile for Q. 'That's really rather good. Put a small case on it, or an envelope containing a document, like the one you're carrying.' He plucked the thick envelope from Bond's hand, dropping it on the tray. 'Now, come over here.' He indicated that Bond should follow him to a wall monitor which showed the large circle of the plate with the sausage shapes of the French stick poking from each end. Now, you could also see the envelope. The latter was not simply a shape any more. It was possible to read the document that faced downwards.

'See?' Q nodded. 'You can read it as plain as the nose on my face.'

There, quite clearly on the monitor was the first page of his flight tickets. Q read off the details – time of flight, number, number of Bond's confirmed seat.

'That's amazing.' Bond turned back to the tray and reached out for the French stick.

'Don't touch that, for heaven's sake!' Q all but shrieked.

'Why, what is it?'

'That's my lunch.'

In all, it was nearly six days before Bond boarded a flight to St Petersburg.

Natalya's journey was a nightmare. At first she thought she had been lucky, a train for St Petersburg arrived at the little country halt only an hour after she had got there and sold the dog team and sled to the official whose job it was to be present for every train that passed through. There would not be another train for two days, he told her, and this one would not even have stopped if he had not been there to hang out the lamps and go through the usual procedures.

She did not haggle over the price of the dogs, selling them for just over the price of her ticket. At least she had no money worries. Natalya was a great hoarder of cash, and as they were paid in hard currency – which meant dollars – she knew that she would be able to buy clothes and almost anything else she needed once the train arrived in St Petersburg. A day later and she thought the train would never get her there.

It was crowded and stank of unwashed bodies. The older people seemed to make the best of it, but some of the young people, she thought, were dangerous. They looked like street hoodlums so she remained for the most part in the one big car which had the most elderly people sitting out the endless uncomfortable trip.

She did not want anyone to see the hard currency, or even the official papers she carried which not only showed her rank as a computer scientist, but also the fact that she had been working at the Severnaya Station. While still on her way by dog sled, Natalya had come to the conclusion that she knew far too much for her own good. She knew who had been behind what had happened – after all she had heard everything and seen the results.

Though much had changed in Russia, the authorities still had rights to search a suspected person, even to make an arrest without any warrant. They still spot checked hotels and rooming houses. When she reached St Petersburg she would be able to buy clothes and other personal items. She would be able to eat, but she had nowhere to go, and it was going to be dangerous.

Natalya was more than certain that Boris had somehow survived. If he had come through the holocaust that had been Severnaya Station, he would be using his one main means of communication: a computer. Boris was not the most pleasant of men, but he did have a brain and he would undoubtedly be watching his own back.

She bought tea and some sausage with a piece of black bread from one of the carts which travelled up and down the train, then, after eating, she tried to blot out all her worries with sleep, but she dreamed of the general and the woman colonel she had glimpsed, pursuing her down endless tunnels.

Natalya could not know that early on the following morning her situation in St Petersburg was to become more fragile.

A plenary session of the Russian Defence Council was due to take place, in the Winter Palace at ten in the morning, and the members, led by Defence Minister Viktor Mishkin, were gathered by five minutes to the hour. Patiently they waited for the one missing member.

Mishkin was undeniably annoyed, pacing the huge room with its baroque ceiling and high windows, then going to the table again, drumming his fingers and constantly looking at his watch. As a rule, even senior officers did not keep the Minister of Defence waiting.

He thought about the big room as his eyes wandered around. At one time, he considered, the last Czar of all the Russias had walked in this room. His children had probably played here. Mishkin gave an involuntary shudder. The ghosts of murdered Czar Nicholas and his family seemed to be everywhere.

At ten minutes past the hour General Ourumov arrived, looking quite calm and carrying his omnipresent briefcase.

Mishkin wished him a brief and surly 'Good morning,' gesturing him to take his usual place at the table.

'Please deliver your report, General,' he commanded before Ourumov had even got to his seat.

The General, in an act which was almost one of insubordination, slowly removed his greatcoat and opened his briefcase to draw out a shiny black file marked, in the Cyrillic alphabet, SOVERSHENNOE SEKRENTO. He then began to speak rapidly as though this were something he wanted said and done as quickly as possible.

'As this Council is aware, seventy-two hours ago, a secret weapons system code-named GoldenEye was detonated over the Severnaya Station. As head of the Space Division, I personally undertook the investigation, and have concluded that this crime was committed by Siberian Separatists seeking to create further political unrest.'

He paused, looking at each of the eight members of the Council in turn, holding their eyes in his before he continued.

'After killing all personnel, these criminals activated the weapon, destroying both the facility and any record of their identity.

'Regrettably, the peaceful work, together with the much needed hard currency earnings, of Severnaya has now been set back by several years. There is only one course of action left to me. I tender my resignation as of this moment.'

The men sitting around the table shook their heads, some of them brought fists down hard on the wood, several cried 'No. No.'

When they had quietened, Mishkin turned to the General and looked him up and down, as though signifying that, as far as he was concerned, he would be delighted if Ourumov resigned. When he spoke, his voice was flat and showed no emotion.

'It would seem that the Council does not, after all, want your head, Arkady Grigorovich. Merely your loyal assurance that there are no other GoldenEye satellites.'

'I can certainly give you that assurance, Minister.'

'Good. Now what of the two missing Severnaya technicians?'

Ourumov looked flushed, frightened and stunned. 'Minister . . . I . . . I . . .' tripping over his own tongue. 'I was only aware of one missing . . . er. . . .'

'Two.' The Minister sounded as though he were a teacher catching out some pupil in a lie.

'But, I . . .'

Mishkin held up a hand to silence the general, then looked down at his papers. 'Our people have searched through the rubble. Bodies have been identified – which was not a difficult task for they were all trapped in an enclosed area. Apart from the military guards, of course.'

'Of course, Minister. But. . . .'

'Everyone is accounted for except one technician. Boris. . . .'

'Grishenko, Minister. I have his name here. . . .'

Mishkin glanced up, giving Ourumov a withering look. 'Boris Grishenko, and one other. A woman, it appears. A very talented Level Two computer scientist. Natalya Fyodorovna Simonova.'

'Simonova?'

Mishkin nodded. 'As I say, a very talented young woman. Conversant in French, Italian, German and English. . . .'

'Would have made a good opera singer . . .' Ourumov sounded angry now.

'Also fluent in four different computer languages.'

'Simonova?' Ourumov repeated.

'That is what the body count shows.'

Ourumov took in a deep breath. 'This is news to me, Minister, but I'll investigate the matter personally and immediately.'

'Good.' Mishkin's silky voice became a shade more threatening. 'It would, I think, be presumptuous, General, to blame this incident on Siberian Separatists before the whereabouts of your own people are determined. Do you not agree?'

'Of course, Minister. Thank you for bringing it to my attention.'

Half-an-hour later, Ourumov sat in his office in the Winter Palace, once the show place of St Petersburg. He spoke urgently on the telephone. Already he had alerted security forces, the police who controlled the area around Severnaya, plus the agency heads in all major cities. He had even managed to get a photograph of Natalya from the data base which he kept for his personal use. Now, he spoke to someone else, his voice dropping to a purring whisper.

'Her name is Natalya Simonova . . . Yes. Yes, that's the one. You know her?'

The voice at the other end of the line acknowledged that he knew the girl.

'If we run her to earth, I want you to keep her under control. Kill her if necessary. You can do that for me?'

'Do it? It would be a pleasure, General.'

'Keep in touch. Remember this is very important to all of us.'

'I'm starting the hunt this very moment, General. It's the kind of task I enjoy.'

9

Wade's Ten Cent Tour

James Bond had visited St Petersburg only once before, but that was in the middle of the Cold War when it was still Leningrad, and his memories of the city remained very clear. He recalled its beauty, the sense of history, for this place was founded by Peter the Great, had become Russia's centrepiece, its 'window on Europe'. It was also the cradle of the October Revolution, something a lot of people would now prefer to forget.

On his last visit he had come as an enemy; he knew the score and was aware that anyone could betray him. This time, on arriving at St Petersburg's international airport, he could almost smell the decay and the lack of direction which had come with the downfall of communism. Like many others, he felt that had the changes come from within the Communist Party, Russia would not have been in the freefall, crime and drug infested bankruptcy which stemmed from the sudden collapse of a ruling government.

Instead of surveillance teams, Bond now kept a wary eye out for criminals.

The queue for taxis was made up mainly of well-dressed businessmen – the Western captains of industry trying to cash in on the needs of this emerging new Russia, and make themselves an honest penny on the way.

He spotted his contact just to the right, away from the queue: big, burly and reading a Russian gardening magazine.

As he walked up to the man, Bond smiled and spoke the contact phrase. 'In London, April is a spring month.'

The American accent was almost too obvious. 'What are you? The weatherman?'

Bond scowled, and the American continued. 'Codes, cloak and dagger. That's all gone, pal. C'mon, the car's over there.' He led the way to a piece of scrap metal that had once been a Moskovich, but it was Bond who leaped to open the door with an 'Allow me'.

The American began to slide into the driver's seat, a broad grin on his face until Bond trapped him between seat and door, his pistol – carried onto the aircraft in the special briefcase which shielded it from the magic eyes and metal detectors – jammed into the man's side. 'Now, talk to me.' His face had taken on the granite look of anger.

There was a long silence, then, 'OK. In London, April is a spring month, while in St Petersburg we're freezing our asses off. That near enough?'

Bond shook his head. 'No. Show me a rose.'

'Aw, Jesus H. Christ.' He undid his belt and, while Bond shielded him from onlookers, the bulky American showed him a small tattoo of a rose on his right hip. Under the rose there was one word – *Muffy*.

'Muffy?' Bond asked, then went to the passenger door and slid in beside the American.

'Yeah, Muffy. Third wife.' The American stuck out his hand. 'Jack Wade. CIA.'

'Bond. James Bond, and you know where I'm from.'

'If I didn't know, I would now. You guys never change. Cold War's over, yet you still go around with your codes, your cloaks, your daggers.'

'The idea is to remain as safe as possible. I thought the CIA still understood the meaning of tradecraft, and the fact that we're all still in business.'

Wade started the engine, which coughed and spluttered, then fired properly. It sounded like an old two-stroke lawnmower. 'We do,' he laughed. 'I knew who you were. Thought I'd have some fun.'

'Well, I wouldn't advise it. Keep to the rules and regulations or you might just find yourself sharing a cell with your nice Mr Ames, or worse. I understand the KGB have merely changed their name. With the instability around here, we could all find ourselves back in the business as usual game.'

'Ah, the Great Game as you Brits call it.' He slowly eased the car out into the traffic.

'I haven't heard anyone call it the Great Game recently – except melodramatic authors and journalists.'

Wade lifted his eyebrows. 'OK, Jim. . . .'

'James,' Bond snapped. 'Never Jim, and certainly not Jimbo.'

'OK, sorry. I thought I'd just drive you around so that we can talk. Show you the sights as it were.'

'The car's clean?'

'Except for the exterior and a few Snicker wrappers.' He threw the magazine he had been reading into the back seats. 'You do any gardening?'

'Not if I can help it. Now, you're the local expert so let me hear your words of wisdom.'

'Wisdom isn't really in fashion over here at the moment. They told me you wanted information, I've been ordered to give it to you. So . . . ?'

'So what do you know about Janus?'

'Hey, look at those buildings, isn't this the most wonderful city you've ever seen? Look, the Winter Palace, and there's the Alexander column. You got one like that in London, yes? Some sailor.'

'Admiral Lord Nelson, yes. Mr Wade, don't play the goofy Yank with me. Now, Janus.'

'You could write what I know about Janus on a pin head, James. In a word, zilch, zipsky.'

'That's two words, let's have some more.'

'Seriously, there are very few on the subject of Janus. Nobody claims to have seen him. That's because they'd be admitting they knew him, but there's no doubt that he's connected. He has lines into government, the military, even the Russian Intelligence Service – a rose by any other name: KGB. Also, the rumour is that he lives on an armoured train.'

'An armoured train? Like the ones so popular with the leaders of the Revolution?'

'I wouldn't know about the Revolution, but that's the story.'

'Where the devil would he get an armoured train?'

'Easy. You can get almost anything if you can afford it. As you're taking Jack Wade's ten cent tour of Petersburg, let me show you a couple of things, before you check in to your luxury fifty-one star hotel.'

Wade drove them down the Nevsky Prospekt, across one of the many bridges and onto the aptly named Across-the-Neva Avenue. From there he headed out into sub-urban St Petersburg, making occasional comments – 'See that decaying pile of buildings?' Flapping a hand in the direction of a series of large block-like structures. 'That was one of the largest military barracks in this city. It just got left when the Sovs were still in power, and it's gone to pieces since the communists were outlawed, because there isn't enough money. When the boys came back from Afghanistan there were just not enough barracks or housing for them – veterans home from the war. That place could have kept a regiment. They just let it fall apart.'

Later, he told Bond that the Hermitage – the world-famous museum of art: part of the Winter Palace – had grave problems, not the least of which was serious rising damp.

'They've also got the Germans and the French demanding their paintings back,' Bond nodded. 'And most of the stuff didn't belong to Germany anyway. All plundered from Nazi-occupied Europe and then plundered by the Red Army when they moved into Berlin.'

Finally, almost out into the country, Wade stopped his ancient car and led Bond over to the top of a high embankment from where they could look down on a huge railway siding.

The buildings, loading bays and platforms were in a state of decay, but the actual railway lines seemed clean and clear of debris.

'A military depot,' Wade explained. 'This was the Petersburg area ICBM marshalling yard: the place where they loaded those intercontinental ballistic missiles that used to have us worried – the ones they ran around the country on trains so they were rarely in the same place twice. They also took them out to silos from here as well.'

'This where Janus gets his armoured train?' Bond's voice took on a serious tone.

'There's a lot of old rolling stock around, yes. Most of the moving missile trains were heavily armoured. They also had armoured carriages for important military and political figures, so they could travel in the proverbial lap of luxury.'

During the return journey, back to the centre of the city, Wade gave him a huge grin. 'Show you something else, Jimb . . . I mean James. Little place they call Statue Park.'

Like the railway depot, it was on the outskirts of the city: a park in name only. Yes, there were trees, and at one time the place had probably been a small park, for there were also a couple of benches, but no formal paths.

At first, Bond thought it could be an exhibition of modern sculpture, but as they left the car, he saw that the sculpture was not modern, nor was it in its finished state.

Strewn between the trees, scattered around the more open spaces he saw statue upon statue, symbol upon symbol, ruined, broken, ripped from plinths, dragged from original sites, carted here and dumped like trash thrown into a land fill. The statues were of people like Marx, Lenin – there were a lot of Lenins – and great metal or stone hammer and sickle emblems. They came in different sizes, from very large to medium. He thought that any active communist could pick up anything from a small to extra large Lenin.

On one of the medium Lenin statues – done in bronze – someone had spray painted an instruction in Russian. Even if Vladimir Ilyich Lenin had been alive, it would have been anatomically impossible for him to obey that particular order.

'You see, James,' Wade grinned, 'when Yeltsin outlawed the communist party, people could not go out and shoot or beat up the old communist leaders. So they were forced to do the next best thing.

'They toppled all the icons of the communist regime.

Lenin, Marx, even the odd Stalin who should have been moved long ago anyway. Statues in stone and metal. The people went out and threw them down – pushed, pulled, used bulldozers or tow trucks. It was a real mess. Then the city began to clear things up. They dumped all the statues in this crummy little park close to the municipal land fill. The trees here were to shield visitors from the fetid horror of the City Dump Number Four. Now they're not bothered by people seeing this stuff.'

'It certainly wouldn't bother me.'

Wade grinned again. 'You know what's funny, James? Real funny. There are people in this very city who think the current administration stinks. People who will not walk past this place, because there are some old statues of Stalin buried here, even though he was condemned after his death. I've heard people say about Boris Yeltsin's regime, that things were better under Stalin.'

Bond shrugged. 'I've heard people in England say they were happier in World War II than they are now under incompetent government. They say, "In the war, we at least knew where we stood." I know what they mean.'

'Strange life, James. Strange old life.' Wade flapped his hand at a swarm of flies that were gathering.

Back in the car, driving to the hotel, Bond dragged him back to the subject of Janus.

'You want to hear what else I know about Janus?'

'Zilch,' you said.

'Sure, well the truth is that *you* don't find this guy. He finds *you*. The only thing I can do is point you in the general direction of his main competition. Nowadays they got one of those keep-your-friends-close-and-your-enemies-closer kind of things going. Jeez, it really is like the old style Mafia here. I sometimes think they've all seen Brando doing his Godfather bit.'

'OK, who's Janus' main competition?'
'A real old KGB guy. Got a bad limp. Right leg. Name of Zukovsky.'
'Valentin Dimitreveych Zukovsky?'
'You know the guy?'
'I gave him the limp.'

Natalya risked the first hard currency store she could find. At least, she thought, I'll know if they have the dogs really close on my heels or if it's only the militia, the police, and the intelligence people.

She had used the public bathrooms at the Moskovsky Vokzal Railway Station as soon as she arrived and the soap she had been given was not quite as bad as she expected, but that was probably because she had tipped the bath lady one precious green dollar.

With her body clean and hair washed, she had eaten at the little cafeteria near the station exit. The coffee was like dishwater, but at least it was hot, and the sandwich of black bread and goat's cheese was tasty. After the meagre meal, she had headed straight out for the hard currency store. She needed a good thick skirt, changes of stockings and underwear, a couple of pairs of jeans, some warm shirts, toiletries, an airline carry-on bag and a large leather shoulder bag.

Natalya had no idea where she was going to spend the night, but that could wait. She had thought of getting a train to Novgorod, then a local to where her parents still lived on the shore of Lake Ilmen, but she knew that it could put her father and mother at risk. If they were looking for her, the first thing they would have done was to put a team of surveillance people onto the house. Better to stay away than risk the rest of her family.

In the women's crowded changing room, she put on

new clothes. Her fur coat, hat, gloves and the leather boots were acceptable, but she carefully checked her papers, moving them into the shoulder bag, together with things she would need. The remainder of her clothes, including those she had been wearing, went into the carry-on. As she was checking her papers, she remembered the official-looking document she had been given over a year ago when she had gone on special assignment to collect computer hardwear. Until now, she had forgotten its existence. This could be useful.

She tied her hair back into a severe bun and looked at the general effect. It would work, she thought, as she was jostled by a couple of other women in front of the one long mirror. This pair was safe enough – fat officials' wives out on a spending spree. They had eyed her too closely to be surveillance people, and she had caught the jealous look one of them had flashed at her when she stood half naked, revealing her slim firm figure.

Out on the streets again, in the Gostiny Dvor arcade – the *Merchants' Arcade*, St Petersburg's main shopping area – she window-shopped until she found a store selling computers. The window-dressing did not bode well. Out-of-date IBMs and Apple Macs, with tiny hard drives, obsolete chips and a minimum of RAM took pride of place.

Natalya breathed deeply and walked into the store.

Out of the corner of her eye she saw the manager looking her over and not putting her very high on the food chain. He hesitated as she looked at the primitive machines, then, as she moved a pace towards the door, he came up to her and asked 'Yes?' in a tone he almost certainly reserved for menials.

She wrinkled her nose, as though indicating that both the manager and the wares on show were giving off the scent of spoiled fish. 'Are these all you have?' she asked.

Sarcastically, the manager raised his eyebrows. 'How many do you want?'

She dug her hand into the big shoulder bag, consulted the influential-looking document. 'Well, twenty-four for the American school, eleven for the Swedish. They must be IBM compatible, with at least 500 megabite hard drives, CD-ROM and 14-4 modems. We have to keep them in line with the ones they already use.'

The manager's attitude switched from disdainful to fawning. 'We are talking hard currency here, yes?'

'What other kind is there?'

'If madam requires a demonstration. . . .'

'Madam requires one demonstration model, and a quiet place to test it for an hour or so.'

'Of course.' He snapped his fingers at a junior salesman and together they led her through to the back of the store where an up-to-date 486 was set up on a spacious desk.

'Just leave me alone. The order will depend on what I find here. I need peace,' booting up the machine as she spoke.

Almost before they were out of the room, her fingers started to fly over the keys. She was on-line and typing in TO madvlad@mosu.comp.math edu – URGENT YOU CALL NATALYA @ 3422-589836.

Then she waited. If Boris had lived following the disaster, he would have managed to get access to a computer by now. He was not a whole man unless he was surfing or listening out.

Nothing.

The minutes ticked away, and with them the optimism.

Her computer beeped and there he was, on screen – or at least a wild cartoon graphic of him. The screen cleared

and the message ribboned out – THOUGHT YOU
WERE DEAD.

She smiled and could have wept with happiness as she
replied – OURUMOV KILLED EVERYONE. FIRED
'PETYA' AND TOOK GOLDENEYE.

It took a couple of minutes, but the answer slid back
onto the screen – YOU AREN'T SAFE. TRUST
NOBODY. MEET ME TOMORROW SIX PM
CHURCH OF OUR LADY OF SMOLENSK.

She had a day to wait. Now all she had to do was find
somewhere to sleep without being wakened by some cop
putting handcuffs on her wrists.

'Do you ever stop talking, Jack?' Bond was fast becoming
irritated with Jack Wade's constant patter.

The Grand Hotel Europe had provided Bond with a
good bedroom and decent food. There were also extras
which he constantly turned down. They even called his
room on the in-house telephone. 'You want a nice friend
for the night?' most of them would say. Bond was very
polite, but eventually took the telephone off the hook.

Wade had picked him up in the Moskovich promptly at
nine. They had spent much of the morning touring the
city and taking odd detours, many of which could prove
helpful.

'Do I ever stop talking, James? Rarely. You needed the
grand tour, so I'm giving it to you. St Petersburg is an
excellent example of a cross-section of the new Russia.
See, the homeless on the streets. . . .'

'Roughly matches that of your own inner cities in the
States.'

'Oh, been to London lately, James?'

'Yes, and New York, also DC. I think you have the
edge on the homeless situation.'

'Look more carefully, friend. The Russian Federation has the real edge. As well as the homeless and hungry, you can see a kinda blurred mirror image of the West. The expensive cars, suits, dresses. On one level these people have learned a lot.'

'They do seem to have learned about the unacceptable face of capitalism, I'll give you that.'

'They've also learned about the unacceptable crime of capitalism. It may be bad in the States, but here it is really a going concern. I did tell you how I got into gardening, didn't I?'

'Several times, Jack. Now how about showing me what I really came here to see?'

'It's OK, James.' He turned into a side-street in which even Bond would hesitate to walk alone at night.

'Very pretty.' He saw the dismal faces and hungry eyes staring from doorways and windows. At the end of the street, a couple of whores made to approach the car as it slowed down. Jack Wade shouted a fast line of Russian abuse at them and they jumped back quickly.

'I know those words,' Bond smiled. 'Only I haven't heard them spoken before.'

'Very necessary, James. Now pay attention, we're coming to an interesting area. As we make a right here, take note of the building on your left.'

Bond sat back, his eyes flicking towards the sign above the doleful-looking shop, reading aloud, 'Kirov's Funeral Parlour. I suppose you're going to tell me this is the dead centre of St Petersburg.'

'Very droll, James. That's the place I was telling you about. Four o'clock this afternoon, the hearse comes in through those big wooden doors next to the shop. They do the business and the hearse is out in ten minutes. I can put the word out if I don't hear from you by three.'

'Makes sense. Good insurance is hard to find.'

'Sure, hang on, we've got to take a left here, then your eyes'll pop.'

The battered old car swung into a broad alley and Bond saw a sight so bizarre he could hardly believe it.

Several expensive cars were parked along the street. Handfuls of well-fed, very well-dressed, smooth-looking Russians leaned against the cars. Less kempt men stood against walls, their wares spread out at their feet. In the boot of every car, the back of every truck, and along the pavement, weapons were stacked: AK-40s, grenade launchers, hand guns, Uzi and H&K sub-machine guns; boxes of ammunition.

Jack Wade grunted, then assumed his role of tour guide. 'Welcome to the shopping mall of death. The wild East. This, for Russia, is capitalism's finest hour. One size maims all, and everyone can make a killing. Kinda like East LA, right?'

'I'm happy to say I've never been to East LA.'

'Well, good for you, James. Hang on, we turn right at the top of this nice little market place. Zukovsky has a joint here, at the end of the street.' He pointed to what appeared to be the entrance of a night club. 'By ten at night, this place is really jumping, but your old friend does his business by day.' He turned right into the alley which seemed to be deserted. 'Your best way in is through any of the doors on this side. Just get in and follow the smell. You'll find him soon enough.'

He pulled over to the kerb, and Bond was out of the car and into the shadow of a doorway long before Wade had even put the car in gear.

The wall, and the doors, made the place look like an abandoned warehouse, but he had seen many places like this: shells built around existing, well constructed places.

He reached for his wallet, and pressed hard on one of the metal protective edges. A secret compartment opened up to disclose an entire set of lock-picking tools. He wondered if Valentin Zukovsky was still as careful about locks as he used to be, back in the bad old days when he worked for the KGB. At that time, Zukovsky had a mania for unbeatable locks and the most sophisticated electronic alarm systems.

It seemed that his old adversary had lost his cunning. Bond was through the door and making his way silently up the stairs in three minutes flat. Above, in the distance, he could hear someone singing just off-key enough to be grating on the nerves.

Valentin Zukovsky was big: tall, broad shouldered and with an elephantine girth. He had a moon face, so much so that people said he must be related somehow because he had all the craters and pock marks to go with it.

His club, which was simply known as Valentin's, was luxurious in an old-fashioned, red plush, gold-fringed manner. At this moment there were several people sitting around obviously doing business of one kind or another. Judging by the type of people talking as low as they could, the business was, if not criminal, certainly bordering on the breaking of laws.

Zukovsky wore a creased and crumpled white suit which looked a size too big for him until he stood up and revealed that its voluminousness was necessary for his bulk.

Half-a-dozen scantily dressed young women waited on tables and pointed out certain favours they could bestow if you ordered from the reverse side of the menu. The most innocent of these was a normal massage.

On a raised dais at one end of the room, another young woman, very attractive and clad in red sequins, battled with 'Raining in Baltimore' by Counting Crows, but she could not quite make the song come to life. It was possible that, apart from being hampered by not being able to carry a melody, she did not understand the words.

Zukovsky had spent the past hour with a reedy-looking, ferret-faced Pakistani arms dealer of very doubtful provenance. They closed no deals, and the Pakistani was just about to leave when Zukovsky suddenly focused his attention on a small TV monitor, about the size of a playing card, set into the table where he always sat. The monitor gave out a tiny beep and the picture came on. Zukovsky glanced down, then did a double-take as he saw who had entered by picking a lock to one of the side doors. He smiled as the picture followed the intruder slowly up the stairs, and his smile became almost benevolent.

Lazily, he gestured to a man who had the makings of a pair of gorillas, and said something to him. He then stood and walked with his lumbering limp towards a pair of red velvet curtains to the right of the dais where the singer was losing her battle with the song.

He passed through the curtains and showed no surprise when the muzzle of an automatic pistol was laid coldly on his neck, just behind the ear.

'Ah,' he breathed as though in a kind of bliss. 'I know only three men who have used that particular brand of firearm, and I've personally killed two of them.'

'That's lucky for me, then, Valentin,' James Bond whispered.

He did not even sense the other man until it was too late. A blackjack came down with a soft thud and Bond fell into the darkness of unconsciousness.

'No, not lucky for you, Mr Bond,' Zukovsky purred.

10

Wheeling and Dealing

Coming back to consciousness was like dredging his way through mud. He was aware of someone talking, and knew what had happened long before he allowed his body to reveal that he was back among the living. It was one of those tricks Bond had learned over the years. If you regain consciousness with your captors nearby, hold back; assess the situation before doing anything.

He heard Zukovsky giving orders, and decided there were at least four people in the room. In the background he could hear the off-key singer trying to get through 'Memories'.

He stirred, shook his head violently and looked around. He was not restrained in any way, and sat in an overstuffed armchair that had seen better days.

Valentin Zukovsky straddled a chair in front of him and there were at least three of his men in the room. Away in the club, the red sequined girl was murdering Lloyd-Webber.

Valentin's face split into a wide and happy grin. 'So, here we are, the great Mr James Bond: dashing, sophisticated secret agent. I'm tempted to be melodramatic and say, so, we meet again.' He chuckled and his men followed his lead, taking their cue from the boss.

'The great James Bond,' he laughed again, and the chorus joined in. 'Shaken not stirred, Mr Bond?'

In the background, the singer hit a particularly terrible high note. 'Who's strangling the cat?' Bond asked.

Zukovsky's initial response was to unholster a pistol and put a shot directly between Bond's legs. A jagged gash speared through the leather upholstery, and dirty white stuffing flew into the air as Bond pressed himself back in the armchair.

'That's my mistress, Irena.' Zukovsky hafted the pistol as though tempted to put another shot after the first, but slightly higher.

'And a very talented girl she is, Irena.' Bond smiled innocently, and Zukovsky seemed to relent, raising his voice and shouting, 'Irena! Take a hike!' The warbling stopped, followed by a number of Russian obscenities and the sound of Irena's shoes clicking off into the distance. Zukovsky winced at the fast and angry tap of the footsteps. Then he turned his attention back to Bond.

'So, what is it that brings you into my neighbourhood, Mr Bond? Still working for the Secret Intelligence Service? Or have you decided to drag yourself into the twenty-first century?' The moon face looked almost friendly. 'Incidentally, I hear that your new boss is a girl. She send you to see me?'

'No, I came to you to ask a favour.'

Zukovsky chuckled again and turned to his bodyguards. 'He wants me to do him a favour.'

They all chuckled, and Bond thought they might be taking their lines from an ancient B movie.

'Bond,' this time he was not looking so benign, 'my

knee aches every day. Twice as much when it's cold, and do you realise how long winter can be in this part of the world?'

He snapped his fingers at one of the thugs. 'Tell him, Dimitri.'

The large bodyguard began to mumble, revealing that he was not blessed with a high IQ.

Zukovsky sighed and shut off Dimitri's muttering with a withering look.

Bond fixed his eyes on his old adversary. 'You know, Valentin, for an ex-KGB man you sometimes surprise me. Surely, someone of your stature must have realised the skill wasn't to hit your knee, but to miss the rest of you.'

Some twenty seconds went by before Zukovsky took it in. 'So why did you not kill me?'

'Let's call it a professional courtesy.'

Zukovsky lifted his big head and growled, 'Then I should return the courtesy.' The pistol came up and he fired, the bullet slamming into the chair about half an inch from Bond's right knee.

'Kirov's Funeral Parlour. Four o'clock this afternoon,' Bond spoke very quickly as though trying to beat a second bullet.

'Really?' The Russian slowly untangled himself from his chair. 'I think we'd better talk about this in privacy.'

After the red plush and velvet of Zukovsky's club, his office was a surprise: neat, modern furniture and filing cabinets; a computer on a large uncluttered desk and coffee brewing in a big state-of-the-art coffee machine.

He gestured Bond into a chair and filled two cups of coffee. 'If my memory serves, you take it black with no sugar.'

'Your memory's very good.'

'Like you, James Bond, my memory was for many years one of my most important weapons.'

Above the desk was a framed portrait of KGB head-quarters in Dzerzhinsky Square. Bond nodded at it. 'You still cling to the old days, Valentin.'

'It's still Moscow Centre.' He settled himself behind his desk. 'The Americans have a saying, "what goes around comes around".'

'True enough.'

'I have a firm belief that we'll all be back in business within a decade. Political ideologies do not die so easily, nor are they simply rubbed out by a declaration. Now, what's this about Kirov's funeral parlour?'

'Two hundred pounds of C-4 explosive, hidden in a coffin. Your man drives the hearse in, the money changes hands, their man drives the hearse out.'

'So?'

'So, their man is going to be arrested and the explosives will be seized. Armed with this knowledge, your man can make a miraculous escape with the money intact. You have time to warn him, and I promise you this *is* going to happen. Also, if certain people don't hear from me by three this afternoon, it all goes down the drain. Explosives, their man, your man and the cash.'

Zukovsky's big head nodded. 'So, what do I owe for this piece of information?'

'Very little. I want you to set me up with Janus.'

The Russian made a little noise, half grunt half laugh. 'And what's Janus done to deserve you?'

'He stole a helicopter.'

'I have six. . . .'

'You have three, and none of them fly.'

Zukovsky laughed. 'Who's counting?'

'Valentin,' Bond was serious now. 'These people aren't

simply criminals. They're traitors. They used that heli-copter to steal a nuclear space weapon. They also killed a number of quite innocent people while they were at it.'

'What else can you expect from a Cossack?'

'Who?'

'This Janus. I've never met him, but I do know what he is – a Lienz Cossack.'

'The Cossacks who fought for Hitler against the Rus-sians in what you called the Great Patriotic War?'

'And you call World War II? Yes, you know your his-tory. When the war was over, the Lienz Cossacks were captured by the British in Germany. They expected to join the British forces and go to war again to obliterate the communists. Instead, the British betrayed them. They were sent back to Stalin, who promptly executed them. Wives, children, the entire families.'

'That's a rather simplistic view, but basically it wasn't exactly our finest hour.'

'You're right, of course. The plain, cut and dried story is simplistic. They were a ruthless people. In the end they got what they deserved. The families were the innocents though. Now, Janus?'

'I'd like you to contact him. You must have ways. Let him know that it's me, and that I'm asking around about the helicopter. You could, possibly, say that we're meeting at the Grand Hotel Europe tonight. Might just drag him out.'

'And you and I are even, while he'll owe me one.'

'Precisely.'

Valentin Zukovsky rose and limped to the door. 'If you're ever contemplating a change of career, let me know.'

At the door, Bond said, 'With people like you around, Valentin, I think I'll always find work.'

*　　*　　*

Natalya's watch had stopped when the pulse of the nuclear explosion had hit at the Severnaya Station. She discovered the fact while on the train to St Petersburg, and it had deeply saddened her, for the watch was of great sentimental value. Her parents had gone without a number of luxuries to purchase it as a gift before she went to university. It would have been easy for Natalya to buy a new one at the hard currency shop, but somehow she did not want to part with it. Maybe she could find a watchmaker who would repair it for her. In the meantime she would rely on public clocks, for the watch felt somehow comforting strapped to her wrist.

On the previous evening she had found a small hotel off Tchaikovsky Street which did not require to see passports and any other identification as long as you paid, in advance, with hard currency. The fact that the salaries at the Severnaya Station were issued in American dollars, a great incentive to remain silent about the work, had become the one most important method of survival – and she thanked God for it.

She had slept late, checked out of the hotel and walked the streets, visiting places which interested her, in order to get through the day. The first thing she did was to go and walk past the church of Our Lady of Smolensk – a tiny blue-painted Orthodox church, out near the Smolny Institute. There she discovered that she had started to think like a criminal, or at least a fugitive, for she checked the exits and entrances, together with all the adjacent streets and alleys.

At around ten minutes to six that evening she was back, looking at the church from the outside. Once more she walked around the building before venturing inside.

It was a little jewel, with icons that took her breath away. Just being in the church stirred her emotions. She did not know if she believed in God, or all the other things associated with the Russian Orthodox Christian religion, but, once inside, with the scent of incense in her nostrils she had a great desire to pray.

She walked slowly down the centre aisle to a large icon of the Virgin Mary, Our Lady of Smolensk, slid a bill into the little box and lit a votive candle, then she knelt to pray.

She prayed for her parents, for the souls of all her friends who had died at Severnaya Station. Then she prayed for herself and a deliverance from the danger in which she now found herself. Nobody had ever taught her to pray, but it came naturally to her, like walking or speaking to a friend. Lastly she added that God's will should be done, then realised that she had been inside the church for a good ten to fifteen minutes. Boris had not shown up and panic leaped into her head like some terrible vision. She began to question everything. Had Boris been caught? Had he led her into a trap?

The panic deepened and she moved back up the aisle towards the west door. Halfway up the aisle she stopped, turning quickly. Was that a noise? Soft footsteps from behind? She saw the flames of votive candles in front of the icon moving, as though someone had passed by them quickly.

The fear gripped her again; she turned towards the door and began to run. Straight into someone who had slipped into the church.

'Natalya!' said Boris.

'Boris!' Her heart was pounding. 'Boris, what's . . . ?'

He put a finger to his lips. 'Quick. Come with me. There isn't much time.' He grabbed at her hand, and for a second she remained uncertain, pulling away, then finally going with him, feeling his arm circle her shoulder as he led her towards a curtain to the right of the icon of Our Lady of Smolensk.

He still held her tightly as they pushed through the curtain, then stopped.

For a split second she could not believe it. She looked at Boris and then at the woman, Xenia Onatopp, who stood just inside the curtain, looking like some terrible harbinger of death.

She tried to shake herself free, felt the needle stab through her clothing into her right shoulder, saw the world spinning, and the terrifying face of Xenia, mouth open as though she wished to devour her. Then darkness.

Boris grinned at Xenia. 'Silly little goose,' he said.

'Let's get her in the car. I've got another appointment,' Xenia spoke with an undisguised relish.

There is a spa in the basement of the Grand Hotel Europe, designed in some way similar to those Turkish baths that used to be found in London and New York. The only difference was that this spa's designers seemed to have dug into the roots of Russian decor, after the old style, rather than any approximation of Turkey.

In what was once the old Soviet Union, you only found one type of chandelier, in various sizes, as though the State had a monopoly on design – which, of course, was true. Those same standard chandeliers lingered on, elsewhere there were fluted pillars, beautifully carved marble, red plush seats and hangings. There was also an unusually high scent of chlorine in the air.

During the evening you could often find many businessmen swimming in the luxurious pool, or reclining in one of the big steam rooms. In spite of the chlorine it was an admirable place to relax and unwind after a long hard day.

112

Bond was glad that he had got in before anyone else. He wanted to swim and steam away the day's tensions on his own. That was why he had carefully hung a *Closed for Cleaning* sign on the main door at the top of the steps leading down to the pool area.

There were other reasons. He wanted to be alone in the hope that Janus would take up the bait. To this end he had checked out the changing rooms and the steam rooms, particularly the big one decorated with beautiful tiling, the steam billowing and hot around him. As he knifed through the water, his mind began to focus on the events of the day, of his reunion with Zukovsky and the short telephone conversation he had initiated with Jack Wade. Zukovsky had taken up the offer regarding the explosives deal, the large amount of plastique was now in the hands of the authorities, and the money had safely reached Valentin. In turn, this almost certainly meant that Janus, by now, would have his sights on Bond, the tethered sacrificial goat.

He executed a fast racing turn and streaked through the water, breathing naturally and swimming with ease. He felt good. He felt even better as he emerged at the end of the pool close to the columned entrance to the big steam bath. The clouds of steam were moving, wafting, reforming as though a ghost had passed through.

Someone, he thought, had taken the bait and lurked within the steam. Time to open his pores and steep himself within that same steam.

He climbed out of the pool, shook himself, picking up the towel he had left at this end, rubbing it through his hair as he moved towards the archway and into the dense cloud, heading towards the alcove where he had left his robe.

Instinct was everything now. Someone else was here,

in this place. Quite near and lurking with some unholy intent.

He felt the presence though he could not see, then the large pillar came out of the mist, just to his left. He had to pass it to get to his clothes, so he danced to the right, away from the pillar, his head turning left, eyes peering through what could just as easily have been dense cloud or smoke.

He knew, from a hundred experiences of surveillance work, from the countless times he had been a target, and the dozens of times he had searched for a target of his own. He turned left and pounced forward, going low in case his adversary carried a knife. A knife would be the weapon of choice in this kind of situation.

As his hand shot out, he felt his fingers touch flesh, then his entire hand was clasped around another human wrist. He jerked forwards and downwards, dragging whoever it was into the relatively clear air of the alcove where he had left his things.

Xenia Onatopp stood facing him, holding a towel in front of her. A twist of her wrist and she was off balance and sprawled on the floor as Bond dived for his pistol, wrapped in the robe which lay on the small slatted bench.

By the time he turned, she had clambered to her feet. She smiled and slowly allowed the towel to drop from her body. Even though he sensed grave danger, Bond blinked the sweat from his eyes. Xenia naked was every man's fantasy of the perfect woman.

'You don't need the gun, Commander.' Her voice was throaty, almost pleading.

'That depends on your definition of safe sex, Ms Onatopp.'

She moved towards him. Two paces.

'That's close enough.'

'Not for what I have in mind.' She kept coming, lifting her hands to cradle his head. A second later she was kissing him as though she were preparing to slake an unquenchable thirst.

He was unable to resist, her passion was so deep and almost violent. Slowly he pulled her back and, bending his knees, replaced the gun on top of his robe before he began to wind himself around her.

Then, in the deepest of kisses, she bit down hard on his lip. He tried to disengage himself and reach back for the pistol, but she caught him behind the knees with one leg and the ground fell out from under him.

This time she was on him like a lioness, ripping at his bathing trunks, tearing them from him, straddling him and whispering, 'James, are you going to hurt me? Please, hurt me if you have to.'

He struggled, but his body was at odds with his mind. For what seemed to be a long time, they wrestled in an erotic sliding and slithering of wet flesh upon wet naked flesh. Panting. Groaning. Grunting, like two animals, for this is what it was about, the animal instincts of two beasts. Finally he was on top of her and could feel himself sliding and thrusting into her while she goaded him on – 'Hurt me, James. When are you going to hurt me?'

Somewhere in the back of his head he recalled Shakespeare's definition of this – making the beast with two backs. Appropriate. Then, the tiny alarm rang in his mind. He knew they were not alone, and at that moment, Xenia's legs slid around his upper body, pressing on his rib cage. He remembered the broken body of Admiral Farrel back in Monte Carlo a thousand years ago.

He turned his head slightly, starting to fight back as his eyes glanced at his watch and he saw a shape coming out of the steam, just reflected in the crystal.

Xenia Onatopp was squeezing harder now, her feet right up behind his neck, her thigh muscles tightening and relaxing.

'Oh, yes,' she breathed. 'Yes . . . Yes . . . Yes.'

He caught her as her legs relaxed slightly, shifting for a tighter grip. Quickly he used his own body to counteract her scissors hold, flipped over, taking her body with him then, sliding his feet under her, he kicked so that she was forced away, shooting backwards over his head. Her body was airborne for a moment, flying with a combination of her own force and Bond's retaliation. Her heels caught the approaching man straight in the mouth, and he let out a gurgle as blood spouted from his nose and lips.

With a flick of his arm, Bond pushed Xenia out of the way and hammered the would-be assailant in the face. The man's feet left the ground for a second and he smashed against the wall with a crunch that made Bond wince.

He turned. 'No. No . . . No . . . No. Stay just where you are, Xenia,' the gun once more in his hand. 'We've had enough foreplay. Now, tell me who sent you and your poor oaf of a friend?'

'Who do you think?'

'I'd bet on Janus.'

'Well, your bet would pay off at a hundred to one. Of course, Janus.'

'Take me to him, then.'

She relaxed for a second. 'Just as you are, or will you meet him with clothes on?'

She said they would meet in Statue Park, then went on to explain what Statue Park really was, going into a lot of details. Bond pretended he was hearing all this for the first time.

She did the monologue lying on his bed, her hands and feet tied with two of his own neckties, a third linking the hands and the feet. Trussed up like a chicken. Even in her surly mood she had tried to make a joke about knowing that he must like bondage. He had put on his robe and found her clothes, an old pair of jeans and a shirt which she wore under a robe she had obviously brought down to the spa. They had gone up to his floor in the lift, very close to one another, for he had a restraining lock on one arm and his automatic jammed into her ribs. He finished dressing, then untied her –

'OK, take me to him.'

She drove and Bond kept the pistol in view to discourage her from doing anything stupid. So, finally they pulled up at the extraordinary pile of broken and discarded icons. The outward and visible signs of a political ideology which may or may not be finished.

'This is it?'

'Yes.' Any trace of the former sexually charged Xenia had disappeared.

'Well, my dear, I've had a lovely evening. Was it good for you?'

'The pleasure was all yours.'

'Please understand if I don't call you.'

'I'm not going to lose any sleep over that.'

He shifted in his seat, and for a second she must have thought he was going to kiss her. Instead his left hand came down with its leading edge hard on that particular point just behind her right ear. He did not have to hit her again. Her mouth opened at the stab of pain then she slumped forward onto the wheel.

'Sweet dreams,' he said and climbed out of the car to find himself staring at the base of a statue of Felix – Iron

Felix – Dzerzhinsky, founder of what would eventually become the KGB and was now the RIS.

He took two steps into the so-called park and through the detritus of the heroes of the Revolution, glimpsed the silhouette of the *Tigre* helicopter and a human shape, which flitted in and out, behind the broken statues.

Slowly he pulled his pistol and walked towards the helicopter. He had taken four steps when the figure came into sight again: a man, walking calmly into a clearing. Nearby there was the sound of a train. Then, as moonlight fell across the clearing, the man walked into sight and Bond saw the grotesque face: the left side marked by a skin graft, and his mouth, on the same side, frozen. The voice was all too recognisable.

'Hello, James,' said Alec Trevelyan.

11

The God With Two Faces

'Alec?' Bond could not believe it at first. He went cold and wanted to vomit, yet his stunned disbelief was gradually turning to anger. He did not need to even ask the question, for he had known Alec Trevelyan as friend and colleague all his active life.

'Yes.' The familiar voice was only slightly slurred by the defect on the left of his mouth. 'Yes, James, I'm back from the dead. I'm not just one of those anonymous crosses on the memorial wall at the SIS headquarters. Does that wall still exist in the new building?' He stopped, as though waiting for a response. 'What's the matter, James? No glib remark? No pithy comeback? You used to be famous for your one-liners.'

'I've got a one-worder for you, Alec.'

'Novel, go ahead.'

'Why?'

'Why? Very droll, James. Why? Because I speak the language well. That do you?'

'No, I think I deserve a decent answer.'

'OK, how about going out, risking life and limb;

bombing around the world, putting your life on the line, then finally ending up on the scrap heap?'

'Happens to everybody, Alec. We're no different from soldiers, civil servants. Name any trade and you come to the same answer.'

'So you think it's OK just to win a war, come home and hear the words, "Well done, chaps. You did a good job, but times've changed. Goodbye." You think that's fair?'

'Nobody has ever said life is fair.'

'Quite. That's it. I went missing because I saw there was no future as a worker ant. I went freelance.'

'You went freelance? Even though you'd taken a pledge. . . .'

'To what? Queen and Country?'

'It was the job we promised to do.'

'Well done, James. Yes, we had made promises, but the world's changed. I happened to move on more or less just in time.'

'The world always changes. That's part of life and part of the job.'

Alec laughed, bitter, with a trace of Biblical wormwood and gall. 'Part of the job? Risk everything, and end up with nothing?'

'Depends on what you mean by nothing, Alec. The world's in constant change. Wars come and go. At the moment it looks as though our old main enemy has gone, but it's left chaos behind. In my job – which used to be your job as well – there's more to do now than at any time. Parts of the old Russian empire are crumbling; there are new terrors, and where there are new terrors, we are most needed.'

'Not in my book, James. I'm happy being a freelance, thank you very much.'

'You'd rather cause the chaos than try to stop it?' Bond raised his hand and the pistol came up with it.

'Oh, James, put that peashooter away. Do you really think that I haven't anticipated your every move?' He turned and began to walk away.

The man, Bond considered, had gone too far to be brought back. The explosion? Ourumov's bullet? Whatever had happened after the operation in the eighties? 'I trusted you,' he said aloud.

'James, don't be so bloody melodramatic. I always took you for a realist.' Trevelyan turned back, coming closer. 'Trust?' he asked, mocking Bond's tone. 'Trust's disappeared, gone, dropped out of the dictionary. The accountants have taken over, or hadn't you noticed? Today's dictator is tomorrow's diplomat; the bomb thrower and terrorist now catch the Nobel Prize. It's all money. We're stuck in the slough of despond which goes under a new name: free market morality. It's a morality where your friends come and go as quickly as the next bus in Regent Street or Fifth Avenue.' He stopped, obviously trying to let his view of life sink in.

'So, how did the SIS vetting miss the fact that your parents were Lienz Cossacks? That, in itself, made you a security risk.'

'They knew, James. They knew everything, they simply thought I was too young to remember.

'We're both orphans. Did you ever think about how the Service prefers orphans? The SIS likes to become your family. Your own parents had the luxury of dying in a climbing accident. Mine survived one of the most treacherous acts perpetrated in the name of the British government. They survived Stalin's death squads, but my father couldn't live with himself, or let my mother live with it. The SIS really thought I would never remember what happened, so it became a nice little irony. The son went to work for the government whose betrayal caused his father to murder his mother, then take his own life. But I always remembered, James. Even when I was being utterly loyal, I never forgot a thing.'

Bond nodded. 'Hence Janus. Well named, Alec. Janus, the two-faced Roman god, come to life.'

Trevelyan's hand came up to the damaged left side of his face. Whether by accident or design he turned so that Bond could see his right profile without blemish, then his left, a scarred and hideous caricature. 'It wasn't God who gave me this face. It was you, James. You set a timer for one minute. . . .'

'And friend Ourumov shot you before time was up. What did he offer you, Alec, a seat on the right hand of God? Am I supposed to feel sorry for doing what was necessary?'

'No, James. No, you're supposed to die for me.'

They stood looking at each other, as though still in the grip of a battle of wills. Then Bond caught a movement to his right, and realised that it was a pencil-thin dot of red light, crawling from his shoulder to his face, then down to his chest. A laser sight. Someone, hidden among the grotesque pile of debris, had him literally in his sights.

Trevelyan turned away again, stopped after three paces and spoke over his shoulder. 'I did think of asking you to join in our little scheme, James. But somehow I knew your loyalty would always be to government orders and not to friends.' He disappeared into the darkness, and Bond moved, falling flat, firing into the darkness, rolling to the right, then jumping up, running again, searching for cover, but the pinpoint of light stayed on him. From somewhere unseen, a sniper squeezed his trigger.

There was a hiss, like lightning cracking through the

air, streaking towards him. He felt a huge blow on his chest, knew somehow that he had been hit by a long range and very powerful stun gun. Once more that day his world went suddenly black and his mind was switched off as though someone had thrown a lever cutting off all thoughts and senses. The last thing he registered was the smell of burning.

He was being banged hard, and regularly, in the back. Someone was calling to him. A woman, her speech accented. He could not move or open his eyes, and his chest felt as though a mule had kicked him.

He tried to retreat into sleep, after all being asleep was being safe, and he had no desire to face anything unsafe.

'Wake up . . . Wake up, Mister . . . Sir, wake up . . . Please wake up.' Definitely a Russian accent, and she seemed to be pounding on his back. Finally he struggled to the surface and found himself returning to a very alien world.

He sat in a cockpit. Rows of instruments and switches were in front of him and a canopy around him, but he was bound into the seat tightly. Rope crossed and recrossed his chest and arms. More rope cut into his wrists and his ankles, while even more was bound around his legs. It did not require genius to realise that he sat, absolutely secured, in the forward cockpit of the *Tigre* helicopter.

The voice, accompanied by banging, came from the rear, electronics/navigation officer's position. 'Wake up . . . Wake up . . .' it droned on like a mantra.

He managed to turn his head just enough to catch sight of the dark hair and attractive face while her feet kept up their pounding on the back of the pilot's seat.

'I'm here. I'm here, it's OK.' His voice sounded slurred and he could feel the parched dryness of his throat. He

123

tried to get his head around so that he could see more, but it was impossible so he concentrated on his restraints which did not seem to give an inch.

'Do something,' the woman was pleading. 'For heaven's sake, do something.'

'I'm a shade tired ... OK.' Pushing with all his strength, Bond managed to reach some of the switches with his face, clocking them on with nose, mouth and forehead. Some of the instruments illuminated and there was a whine as the engine began to spool up, the rotors chop-chopping above them.

A beeping noise attracted his attention and, with the ropes pressing into his flesh causing extreme pain, he leaned forward to peer at the instrument concerned.

It was a flashing display on the weapons' control panel. In red it flashed DELAY LAUNCH IN SECONDS TO ... 17 ... 16 ... 15.

Launch? He thought. Missiles? The chopper itself?

The numbers moved on relentlessly, and Bond wondered if this was his personal countdown to death – for him and the young woman behind him.

... 07 ... 06 ... 05 ... 04.

The whole cabin began to shake violently and his ears popped as, with great streams of flame, a pair of missiles screeched off from under the stubby weapons bearing wings.

The two missiles moved so fast that by the time he had taken in what was happening, they were flickering flames a mile or so in the distance, running low over buildings, and the lights of St Petersburg. Then, in tandem, they lifted upwards, slicing into the sky, crossing each other's trails.

Noises still came from the weapons' control panel. A high-pitched whine, followed by a growl and an urgent

deet-deet-deet sound that he recognised and associated
with a target acquisition warning.

Eyes down again and he saw another counter moving.
One set of figures remained set at 003.109.001. That would
be the target position, and below it another series of
numbers flowed, suddenly stopping at the same co-
ordinates – 003.109.001. A match, and he now knew
where the target was located. He was sitting in it.

Far away, high in the sky to the left, the rockets
had turned and were coming down, like perfectly
aimed arrows, pointing directly towards them. He could
feel the sweat trickle from his hairline as he frantically
looked for the one way of escape. He yelled back at the
girl. 'I need a square red button. Probably lit up. Can you
see it?'

'There . . . To your right . . . To your right. . . .'

His eyes flicked over and there it was with the words
CAUTION EJECT above it, and out of reach.

With a final thrust, summoning all his strength and backing it up with a yell, he slammed his head towards the
button and felt his right temple touch. Then the world
changed again.

The rotors howled and were thrown away from the helicopter. There was a massive thump from beneath the long
cockpit as it was launched into the air, a one-piece cabin
capsule which shot to almost two hundred feet before
parachutes were deployed.

At the apogee of its surge upwards, the capsule seemed
to hover, not moving, in the air, and from below came
the devastating explosion as the two missiles smashed into
the frame of the helicopter, sending up a great fireball
that, for a second, engulfed the capsule.

The girl was screaming behind him, and he knew
that his own mouth was open, but could not tell if it was

wide in a silent scream, or if he was also shrieking with fear.

The capsule drifted down and hit the earth with a heavy, bone-jarring thud. It was several seconds before Bond realised that the jolt of the ejector rockets, combined with the thud of landing, had loosened the ropes. He struggled, pushing and pulling until, finally, his arms were free, then his hands, so that he was able to reach down and release his legs.

He popped the canopy and began to climb out and along to the rear compartment where the girl sat in shock, wild-eyed and white knuckled as she clung to the arm rests of the seat. She was held down by straps with buckles at the back; her arms were secured to the seat, and there was a tight strap around her ankles.

He swung around, unlocking her section of the canopy, reaching out to her – swiftly undoing the straps. 'Come on. Let me help you out.' He spoke gently, though he later realised that he was probably shouting as his ears were popping from the G forces to which they had been exposed during the ejection.

The girl grabbed his arm and he helped her to the soft earth. Almost as they touched the ground, she lashed out, kicking at his shins and trying to escape from him.

'Stop!' He was shouting by now.

'No! Let me go. Take your hands off me!' She clawed at him with her fingernails.

'I'm trying to help you. Stop it now.'

They were still grappling when the white spotlights of two helicopters nearly blinded them from above. Near at hand they could hear the wail of sirens and a voice on a loud hailer unit in one of the helicopters told them in Russian to stay exactly where they were. '. . . If you move, you will be shot where you stand,' the voice continued.

'I think it would be a good idea to pretend we're one of these damned statues,' Bond said, gently wrapping the trembling girl in his arms.

12

Floating Through Sunlight

The headquarters of Military Intelligence for the St Petersburg area lie behind high brick walls near what was once Red Army Student Street. Within the walls the army keeps a large number of vehicles ranging from APCs and the smaller open-topped BTU-152u Command Vehicles, to tanks. The headquarters building is of a dour red brick, in stark contrast with the rest of the city which sports some of the most beautiful buildings and views in the whole of Russia, if not the world. Of all Russian cities, St Petersburg was rebuilt to closely mirror its former glory following the terrible siege of 900 days during the War.

Bond and Natalya were taken straight to an interrogation cell: bare and uncompromising – the metal door slammed and locked behind them immediately. An unshaded light bulb hung from the ceiling and the furnishings were a simple metal table and three metal chairs. The table and two of the chairs were bolted to the floor. The third, Bond immediately discovered, had been brought in recently and was not secured.

129

There was no point in even searching for bugs, for they would be invisible these days without an electronic sweeper and even that would not guarantee results. He would have to risk talking anyway, for he needed to work on the girl and coax her back to normal. At the moment she cowered in a corner, her eyes full of fear.

Moving towards her, he said quietly, 'We haven't much time.'

She crawled along the wall, moving away from him, almost shouting, 'Stay away from me. Don't come near or I'll scratch your eyes out. Just stay away.'

In the end, he managed to grab her by the wrists and pull her towards him. 'Now listen,' he spoke almost in a whisper – not gentle but flat, urgent and cold. 'I work for the British Government. So, you can either take your chances with me, or put your life in the hands of your fellow countrymen – the people who killed everyone at Severnaya.'

'Where's Severnaya? I've never been to Severnaya.'

'Your watch has.' He twisted her wrist, reading off the frozen time. 'Seven-fifteen and twenty-three seconds in the evening. The very moment the electronics everywhere in the vicinity were stopped by the GoldenEye blast.'

'The GoldenEye . . . ?' she began, and he saw that she was starting to relent.

'I'd put money on the fact that you were the one who climbed up the remains of the big satellite dish to get out.'

It seemed an age before she gave him a little nod of agreement.

'Who are you?' he asked.

'Natalya Fyodorovna Simonova. Yes, I am a Level Two programmer, and I know what happened.'

'Natalya, that's a lovely name. Who was the inside man on this?'

'Boris. Boris Grishenko.'

'Russian Federal Intelligence – the old KGB – or military?'

'A brilliant computer programmer, but I think probably old KGB. He acts crazy but he's quite exceptional.'

'Was there anyone else?'

'Inside? No.'

'What about satellites. Are there any more?'

'Just one moment. It's my turn to ask questions.' She appeared to have gained confidence. 'Who are you? Who are you really?'

'James . . .' he began, then a key rattled in the metal door which was thrown open and an armed guard preceded the Minister of Defence, Viktor Mishkin, into the cell.

Mishkin looked suave in a long dark coat with a sable collar over his sober dark suit. In his right hand he carried Bond's automatic pistol, and his smile was the smile of a tiger.

'Well, good morning, Mr Bond.' He held the gun as a child might hold a small flag, wiggling it in the air. 'Sit, both of you.'

Bond immediately grabbed the metal chair that was not bolted to the floor, while Mishkin took the chair opposite.

'In case you do not recognise me, I am Viktor Mishkin, Minister of Defence.' He hardly paused for breath, putting Bond's pistol on the metal table in front of him. 'So, how shall we execute you, Commander Bond? The usual manner: the bullet to the back of the head? Quick, painless and straightaway, now, so we can deny any knowledge of you?'

Bond raised an eyebrow. 'No small talk or chit-chat, Minister? You're not going to do a proper sinister interro-

131

gation? Nobody has time for these things any more. Interrogation's a lost art.'

'This isn't the time to be flippant, Commander. I have one question only. Where is the GoldenEye?'

'I assumed you had it, Minister.'

'No. All I have is an English spy, a Severnaya programmer, and the helicopter they stole . . .'

'You only have what one traitor in your government wanted it to look like.'

Mishkin's hand came down heavily on the table. 'Who is behind your attack on Severnaya? Who ordered it?'

'Who had the access codes?'

'The penalty for terrorism is death, and I regard the pair of you as terrorists.'

'What's the penalty for treason these days, Minister? A slap on the wrist and banishment to a country dacha, like the traitors who bungled the coup in '91?'

'Some died.'

'Supposedly by their own hand. You have another traitor close to you, Minister.'

Natalya suddenly spoke, loudly and with a very firm voice. 'Stop it. Stop it, both of you. You're like children squabbling over their toys.'

Bond looked at her, a smile around the cruel corner of his mouth. 'Didn't you know, my dear? The one who dies with the most toys wins.'

'Stop it. You know the truth as well as I do.' She looked at Mishkin. 'It was Ourumov. General Ourumov and that woman – the one like a snake. Together they killed everyone and stole the GoldenEye.'

Mishkin threw back his head and gave a one note laugh. 'Ha, why would Ourumov do that?'

'Because there's another satellite. Exactly the same as the one they used to destroy Severnaya.'

Mishkin's smile turned itself off, as though someone had thrown a switch. 'This is true?'

'Absolutely true. The second one is code named *Mischa*, and somewhere out there is a second control complex . . .'

A commotion at the door stopped them short. General Ourumov seemed to cannon into the room, slamming the door behind him. He looked unkempt, tired, unshaven and as though he had slept in his uniform. Sweat dripped from his face as if he had been running through terrible humidity and was very out of condition.

'Defence Minister . . . I must protest . . .' he blurted, struggling for breath.

'General Ourumov. . . .'

'This is *my* investigation. You are out of order!'

'From what I've just heard, General, it is *you* who is out of order.'

Ourumov leaned forward and picked up Bond's pistol from the table. 'I think I've seen this weapon before!'

'Put it down, General.'

'In the hands of our enemy. Do you even know who the enemy is, Viktor? Do you?'

Mishkin made a gesture, as though he were knocking an insect out of the way. 'Guard! The General is under arrest. Escort him to. . . .'

The guard, a young soldier in his early twenties, paused for a second, then began to unholster his machine pistol – too late, for Ourumov wheeled and shot him. The guard was thrown against the wall, his chest torn out by the Glaser round.

Bond grabbed Natalya and dragged her down to the hard stone floor, trying to protect her with his body, as Ourumov turned and took off Mishkin's head with a second shot.

'This ammunition takes no prisoners, does it? What a terrible state of affairs. Defence Minister Viktor Mishkin is murdered by the cowardly British agent, James Bond . . .' He worked the slide on the pistol, flipped the magazine from the butt, pocketing the ammunition and tossing the gun to Bond as his hand went towards the weapon holstered at his hip.

'. . . In turn, Bond is shot while trying to escape.' He levelled his pistol and began to shout, almost hysterically – 'Guards . . . Guards. Quickly.'

The pistol came up in his hand, but Bond had already moved, diving for the unanchored metal chair and hurling it at Ourumov, who caught it across his chest, falling backwards, the pistol going off and a bullet ricocheting around the cell. As it happened, so Bond was on Ourumov, his fist catching the general on the side of the jaw so that his head lolled back, unconscious.

Bond dragged Natalya – and the one loose chair – to the wall behind the door just before it clanged open, and two soldiers, both with machine pistols, barrelled into the room, and stopped short, staring at the bodies, completely shaken by what they had found.

Before the pair had a chance to react, Bond leaped forward, swinging the chair – left and right, hard, smashing into the faces of the two men, then catching Natalya by the wrist, he hauled her out of the cell stopping only to scoop up a machine pistol which had fallen from one of the now bleeding and unconscious soldiers.

They were in a long passageway studded with metal doors, like the one belonging to the cell from which they had escaped. At the far end of the corridor, steps led upwards and, still pulling Natalya with him, Bond headed towards them, reckoning that stairs going up probably meant there would be stairs going down. He was wrong.

Damn, he cursed. People on the run in buildings normally go up and he had wanted to break that psychological fact by getting down to a lower floor.

At the top of this short flight of stairs, another long corridor led to an open plan office. Three soldiers stood at the ready in front of the office, and, as he glanced back, he could see Ourumov, puffing and blowing, his pistol unholstered and accompanied by three more men, beginning to follow the fugitives.

He put a quick burst in the direction of Ourumov, and then fired a long burst at the three men in front of the office. He saw one man go down, and another fall onto one knee as though wounded. The third ducked back into the office.

There seemed to be no way out, so he signalled to Natalya, making her flatten herself against the wall as he edged his way forward. Three steps and they came to an archway on their left which appeared to be the entrance to yet another very dark and narrow corridor.

There was no option so he pulled the girl close and asked if she was all right.

'I will be if I live,' she said with some spirit.

'Run like hell and don't stop for anyone.' They set off at a sprint into the darkness.

Light gleamed at the far end and, as they came closer, he deciphered a red notice in Russian which said – NO ADMITTANCE. INTELLIGENCE ARCHIVES LENINGRAD AREA.

'Someone not keeping up with the times,' he muttered. A very stout metal door with a big lock barred their way. 'Keep going!' he shouted back to Natalya, firing a burst from the hip which blew out the lock and set a siren wailing.

They crossed into the archive area and Bond slammed

the door behind them. They were now in a passage leading to a larger well-lit section, and lined with a series of cabinets teetering and leaning in an obviously unsafe manner.

He wished, fleetingly, that he had more time. He would have liked to have a squint at some of the files which were piled in bulk in those units.

As soon as they reached the end of the entrance hallway, he motioned Natalya to stand clear and put his shoulder against the last cabinet. It toppled easily against the next structure and set off a domino effect so that the cabinets and shelving crashed down against the door. Swiftly he crossed the little passage, did the same with the cabinets on that side, then turned his attention to the main archives.

Bond and Natalya found themselves in the uppermost section of three huge circular galleries, with what appeared to be a glass rotunda directly above them. Here things were more orderly. To his right he saw a large round segmented window between the neat and solidly built bookcases that circled the gallery. From behind there was a pounding as Ourumov's men tried to batter their way in.

Moving closer to the window, Bond glanced out to see a view of the military vehicle park far below. Too far. He craned closer to look straight down and wondered if what he had in mind was possible. Then he became aware that the pounding had ceased on the door behind them, making him even more alert. Crossing to the wooden balcony rails he peered over to see Ourumov, flanked by his men, coming onto the gallery below them.

He motioned Natalya to back off silently and get into the window opening, then he looked down again and saw, with a lurch to his stomach, that the floors of the galleries had been built with several layers of strong thick Lucite. He could see to the circle below, and knew it was only a matter of time before Ourumov and his troops would spot them as they peered upwards through the transparent flooring.

As though his thought triggered the action, Ourumov shouted, pointing up at them and bullets began to plough their way into the glass-like floor, ripping and sharding the material.

'Run,' he yelled at Natalya. 'Follow me!' and they set off to circle the entire upper gallery, Bond wildly looking to see if there were any alcove or passage which would make them safer.

As they ran so the bullets stripped out the flooring like several pneumatic drills, following them around the gallery, making it impossible to turn back, for the thick Lucite was already shredding behind them.

Natalya stumbled, half fell, slowing her forward movement. No bullet hit her, but the floor gave way, tearing to pieces behind her, so throwing up her arms and screaming, she fell through the jagged hole, straight into the arms of the soldiers below.

Bond cursed, momentarily wondering if he should drop down and try to save her. She had a great spirit and had already shown that she had the guts and determination to keep going.

He hardly paused, knowing that he would be letting his heart rule his head if he stopped now, for the bullets continued to open up the floor behind him. He would soon be running out of space, for he had almost completely covered the entire ring of the gallery, but four strides ahead he caught a glimpse of a metal safe inlaid between the shelving, with room for him to climb on to it. They would have to blow the thing out from under him with explosives that would wreck the entire building if he could make it.

He judged the distance and then took off, going for a high jump, landing in a heap on top of the recessed safe as the fire from below removed the floor he had just left, and continued to stitch holes in what remained of the gallery.

He saw that he was now almost directly opposite the big circular window which looked down on the vehicle park. He took a few deep breaths, unbuckled the belt Q had given him, feeling for the safety catch and moving it to the off setting, twisting the belt around his right wrist.

Lifting his arm, he aimed at what appeared to be solid stone on the far edge of the rotunda, high above. He took a deep breath, counted to three and pressed the firing mechanism on the buckle.

The belt bucked in his hand as the tine shot out, trailing its high tensile cord. It was over in a flash, but Bond felt it was all happening in slow motion as he held his breath, praying that the tiny piton would hold.

It hit the base of the rotunda with a solid thwack, and one quick pull on the belt told him that it was buried firm and deep into the stone.

Another intake of breath, and Bond took up the slack, then launched himself from the top of the safe, swinging in a wide arc, right across the gallery, straight towards the circular window.

He was aware of the strain on the belt and his arm; of the air cleaving as he swept through it; and, for a second, the long drop down through the other galleries below.

He struck the window in the centre, feet first, letting go of the belt and lifting his hands to cover up his face. Then came the shattering crash as the window caved outwards and James Bond smashed through it, dropping over forty feet to the hard ground. As he went down, he thought of the many good things he had experienced in his life and the last face which crossed the screen of his mind was that of Natalya Simonova. Sadly, in a split second, he thought she might have been the best thing of all. Now he felt as insignificant as a tiny speck of dust floating through sunlight.

13

Track Event

It was probably one of the heaviest bets Bond had ever wagered. When he had stood by the big circular window after they had entered the top gallery of the archives, he had seen, parked directly below him, a military truck with its tarp in place. Nobody was in sight, so he worked out the odds on it having been moved as evens. If it had been driven away during the chase around the gallery, it would be a hard landing bringing at the least serious injury: more probably, death.

A confirmed gambler, he had weighed the odds and, having seen no sign of life around the lorry, had bet on it being in place. So, he came shooting out of the window in a shower of glass and, glancing down, saw he had won. The truck was still in position. It was not the softest landing he had ever made, but it was safe enough and the most difficult part – but for a couple of bruises – was getting down from the top of the tarpaulin to ground level.

Once there, on the hard paved walkway surrounding the Military Intelligence Headquarters, he melted into the shadows, making his way across to the vehicle park.

At some point, he knew, the main gate would have to be opened and he would just have to take his chance. He had very little ammunition left so it was a case of picking the right vehicle. He softly moved up and down the lines, rejecting the small jeep-like scout cars, the APCs and the smaller BTU-152us with their open tops and room for some eight men.

There was movement coming from the main entrance, so he flattened himself against a cumbersome T55 tank, watching as Ourumov and one of the soldiers from the HQ dragged Natalya towards a car and threw her roughly into the back. Ourumov sounded furious and had a weapon in his hand.

Natalya was making a lot of noise as she was pulled to the unmarked black car. She had already taken in the fact that Bond was not lying, crushed and broken, outside the building, so she clung to the hope that her new friend had somehow escaped and was already preparing a rescue. By the time they manhandled her into the car nothing had happened and her optimism began to fade.

Over in in the vehicle park, Bond turned and found himself looking at the rear of the T55 tank. He frowned and wondered, then made up his mind and moved.

Natalya could smell the sour, unwashed body of Ourumov, crammed next to her in the car. The soldier drove, heading for the main gate with its barber's shop red and white poles. They slowed for only the minimum amount of time it took for the guards at the gate to identify Ourumov, then – with the general shouting for the driver to move as fast as he could – they shot out of the gate, rubber burning as the car fishtailed, skidding into a left turn, building up speed as they ran parallel to the wall of the vehicle park.

When it happened, Ourumov jerked and actually cried

out in dismay. The wall on their left seemed to disintegrate and the prow of the powerful T55 lurched through the debris onto the road directly behind them. It slewed from side to side, but still followed, at its flat out speed.

In the car there was a touch of terror in Ourumov's voice as he shouted to the driver to move it. The fear which now came as a stench from the general was founded on an incident during the Afghanistan campaign when he had been in a tank, similar to the T55 that rumbled at their heels. Ourumov's tank had taken a direct hit and the general was only one of two people to get out alive. In his darker dreams he could still hear the screams coming from the rest of the crew as the metal coffin burst into flames. He had shown a not unnatural fear of tanks from that time.

Bond had sighed with pleasure when he fitted himself into the driving seat of the T55 and switched on, pulling the small knob that controlled the starter, hearing the engine immediately bumble into life. He looked around and saw there was a fuel gauge showing full; the rest of his quick course in tank driving was one of trial and error, testing the long metal lever controlling the gears and the thick control column which, he discovered, turned the machine somewhat violently, slowing the tracks on one side and speeding those on the other so that it staggered to left or right. The brakes and accelerator were easy enough to find, and the only problem he faced there was that they were transposed from those of a normal car – brake pedal on a long stalk for the right foot and accelerator on the left. He had no time to examine, let alone use, the array of electronics, but he did know that he could not drive the beast and fire the 100mm gun that sprouted some twenty-nine feet from the turret. There was a machine gun in reach alongside the driver's seat. He could not use that while Natalya was still in the car, so he concentrated on a straight chase. With luck, if he could control the machine, he might just run Ourumov to earth – literally.

What he had not bargained for was the lack of vision through the forward slit. Somewhere within reach there was probably a periscope so that he could view the rear, but, for the time being, he needed all his concentration to learn how to handle a T55. It always looked so easy when you saw those tank battles in movies, but he had quickly discovered that unless you knew what you were doing, the tank had a tendency to drive you rather than the other way around.

He had also not taken in the noise factor. Inside the brute there was a bone jarring vibration from the tracks, and the noise was amplified by the interior which seemed to act as an acoustic chamber. One of the first things he had done on hitting the street was to reach for the driver's headphones and clamp them on, then hit the search button on the radio in the hope of locking on the police band. His Russian would probably be enough to follow any chatter concerning road blocks and the like. The rest was – in the words of an old sergeant major he had once known – 'Brute force and ignorance'.

As well as controlling the tank, dealing with the extreme noise and vibration, not to mention the limited sight lines, he had to watch for the unexpectedly high volume of traffic which was out in force this evening. Twice he had almost squashed a couple of cars, now he saw Ourumov's car take a right and he followed, cutting the corner at an angle so that the tank's hull lifted and there was an unpleasant buckling and crunching sound as he flattened a row of parked cars. As the hull came down again, Bond saw the car had hit an intersection crammed with traffic and was reversing rapidly, touching the sides of other parked cars as it went, sending sparks from the bodywork as it weaved backwards, then taking another right turn into an alleyway.

He gunned the motor and, this time, made a perfect right turn, tapping the brakes and hitting the accelerator with the control column hard over. Too late he saw that, while the alley was big enough for the car, it certainly gave no leeway to the tank. He was committed, though, so he straightened up and increased speed.

It was a bumpy ride as the alley was some six feet too narrow for the T55. This was where the brute force and ignorance came into play, and to his surprise, he found that if the alleyway were too narrow, the tank took care of it, cutting a swathe of brick, dust and rubble from the buildings on either side, jerking and heaving its way along the old cobbled narrow street, finally bursting out onto a wider road – a T-junction with a wide canal facing him. There was nothing he could do but pull the tank around to the left, in a series of jerks and motor noise.

The car had squealed left, and then right, onto a bridge crossing the canal, turning right. He started to make the right turn onto the bridge when he realised that it was impossible. The T55 had carved its way through the alley without any problems, but he could now see, through the smoke and brick dust filtering through the narrow driving slit, the bridge was a delicate and beautiful structure, built to take normal traffic, but a serious hazard for the tank, the weight of which it could not possibly carry.

He was pointing in the wrong direction, the hull swivelled to the right several feet from the entrance to the bridge.

Aloud, he said, 'Let's see how you can manage a one-eighty,' touching brakes, holding the control column far over to the right, then putting his left foot hard down on the accelerator.

It was like a fairground ride. The tank swung around on its own axis, doing a perfect 180° turn, and as it completed the manoeuvre, he saw that the military were already chasing him – a pair of the jeep-like vehicles and two BTU-152us, fully loaded with troops who seemed to be sitting to attention in the long open back.

The two little jeeps had no chance. Their drivers, blinded by the dust and smoke, could not even see as they shot out of the alley exit and ploughed straight ahead, seeing the canal too late. They both tried to fly, which is not a good option in small jeep-like vehicles. They remained airborne for a few seconds, then smashed hard into the dirty water of the canal, their occupants leaping and scattering into the water.

The pair of BTUs made the left turns, very close to each other and were on top of Bond's tank before they knew it. He tried to weave out of the way, but hit one of the BTUs head on, swerved and just touched the side of the other vehicle – which was enough to push the troop carrier aside. As he moved forward at full speed, Bond was aware of men yelling as they were thrown from their stricken six-wheeler.

'Road hog,' Bond muttered, craning forward to see Ourumov's car ahead of him, moving in the same direction, but on the far side of the canal.

Inside the car, the General was panicking. 'For God's sake it's only a slow old tank. Outrun him.'

'I'm doing my best, sir.' The driver was about as happy as the general.

In the back seat, Natalya glanced through the rear window and saw that the tank was making steady progress, almost running parallel with them on the opposite bank.

She smiled with glee, then turned and gave Ourumov a wolfish grin.

The general caught her look, did a double take, his face crimson with anger. 'Shut up!' he barked at her, then saw they were approaching another bridge to their right. 'Over that bridge,' he screamed at the driver. 'Cut in front of him. Over the bridge and straight on. He won't have time to turn quickly. We can lose him.'

Natalya's smile faded as she saw six police and military cars racing up behind the tank on the far side. The police cars were making no secret of their presence – lights flashing and sirens wailing. The military vehicles, Armoured Personnel Carriers (APCs), were bristling with weapons.

Bond saw Ourumov's car pull right, onto the bridge. He floored the accelerator but the tank seemed to be already at its maximum speed and he could see that he could not expect to catch the car before it exited from the bridge and, presumably, head on down a road to his right.

He knew other transport was chasing him, even though he could not see them. The wail of the sirens, though faint in his ears, was detectable and lord knew what else was out there: he pictured APCs with anti-tank missiles which could easily blow him to fragments.

The car shot off the bridge, straight in front of him. Bond slowed, stick hard over and his feet moving between accelerator and brake. This time he had complete control and the tank turned accurately into the street. Ahead he saw the car, held up, waiting to traverse a roundabout in the centre of which stood a huge gleaming statue of Czar Nicholas on a great winged horse.

For a moment, Bond thought he was going to catch up and be able to ram Ourumov's car, but as he approached, so the car made its turn into the traffic flow.

'He who hesitates . . .' Bond muttered and took the

tank straight on and right across the roundabout. Inside his metal capsule, he clearly heard the scream of braking cars and trucks desperately trying to avoid hitting the tank, and he mouthed a curse when the right track sliced into the front of a beer lorry. Some of the load bounced in front of the driver's slit and he wondered what the final damage might be.

But, by this time, he was across the middle of the round-about and felt the crushing bump as the hull hit the base of the statue, depositing the Czar Nicholas, still astride his winged horse, neatly over the long muzzle of the 100mm main gun.

From the back of the car, Ourumov saw what seemed to be an avenging angel bearing down on him. For the first time in years the general made the Orthodox sign of the cross, his eyes wide with fear.

Back at the roundabout, beer cans littered the road – a temptation which proved too much to many of the drivers and pedestrians who leaped into the street to indulge in a feeding frenzy, grabbing at the cans, filling shopping baskets, or using pullovers and skirts as make-shift bags to carry as many of the coveted beer cans as possible.

Traffic was at a standstill and the entire scene was filled with a cacophony of horns and shouts from frustrated drivers: including the police and military.

For a while, at least, Bond was free of the pursuing authorities, but it could not last. More by his instinct than the sirens, he realised that, somehow, more police had got behind him.

If he could have seen the convoy from the air, he would have known that the T55 was close behind the general's car, and three police cars were fast gaining on the tank.

Bond was getting more experienced at handling the

machine with every minute. He took a long, wide bend to the left and glimpsed a low bridge directly in front of him, about fifty yards away, with Ourumov's car putting on speed, just passing under it.

He tried for more power; saw the arch come up, heard the mighty crunch and the bang as the statue hit the overhang, rolling back into the direct path of the pursuit cars.

By now he was starting to pick up communications on the police band. There was talk of setting up a road block with anti-tank weapons and a lot of firepower, though he had no idea where this was being done. It was obvious that it had to be somewhere along the route of the general's car, which he saw, too late, was making a fast right-hand turn.

He slowed, but was too late and rumbled past the street down which the car had now disappeared. They were on the city's outskirts and the housing was starting to thin out, but he slowed, preparing to take the next right turn, hoping against hope that he would find himself running parallel to Ourumov's car.

Piling on the power, listening to the instructions regarding the road block and trying to maintain control of the tank, Bond realised that the next intersection was coming up fast. He slowed and turned right, anxious to see if he would be able to sight Ourumov's car. As he took the right into a wide street, he saw to his frustration that this was a dead end. Facing him was a three-storey office block. There were lights in the street level windows and he saw people moving behind them. At the last minute, people in the office complex heard the sound of the oncoming tank and began leaping for cover as the juggernaut crashed through, turning furniture to matchsticks, typewriters into squashed and mashed metal, and exploding computer screens.

He pushed the power to its maximum, and the tank went right through the building, like wire through cheese. He emerged into a wide street, bursting out from the rear wall of the building, cursing the brick dust and pieces of stone pouring down from the turret. For a second, he had to pull his mind back to the direction he would have to go in order to catch the car. He hesitated, then pulled the machine right and found out exactly what the police chatter had meant.

Facing him was the barricade, complete with a large anti-tank gun and a lot of other firepower. An officer stood in a command car to the right, obviously waiting to give the order. The only problem he had was that Bond's tank had broken through the wall *behind* the barricade.

For the first time, Bond reached for the handle and trigger of the forward firing machine-gun, squeezed and was relieved to find the weapon was fully armed and ready.

He smelled the cordite in the cramped enclosed space of the T55, and saw the utter confusion in front of him. Some of the tracers from the machine-gun were hitting, all of them were causing complete panic in the waiting military unit. He spotted one brave man attempting to swing the anti-tank gun and bring it to bear, trying to turn it to face the rear of the barricade, but the tank was already on top of them. He felt the whole mass of metal tip, heeling over to one side as the right tracks crushed the gun.

There were a few bullets as he moved away down the road, and one armour piercing round did hit the heavy plating on the rear, but he was home free. More than that, he had just caught a glimpse of Ourumov's car crossing the road about two blocks ahead. He did not need to follow closely on its heels now, for he had recognised the neighbourhood. On Jack Wade's tour of St Petersburg, the American had brought him along this road intentionally. He now knew exactly where Ourumov was heading. All he could hope for was that he could get there in time.

14

The Train

This was yet another of the remnants of the old Soviet military machine. It lay deep inside a large oblong cutting, the top of which was surrounded by a crumbling brick wall and razor wire. The buildings were already starting to break up, and there was a strong sinister sense of long gone power about the place.

It had obviously once been somewhere of tremendous strategic importance. You could tell that by the types of structures and the strongly constructed platforms, together with now rusting stubby cranes.

Bond lay in a gap in the wall, on top of the cutting, looking down on the panorama below him; the T55 stood at the end of the deep ruts it had made when climbing up the high sloping grass embankment, and he was relieved that he appeared to have arrived before Ourumov. That had not been difficult, for the car in which the general travelled with Natalya was forced to take normal roads, while the tank had been able to move away from streets, so slew off across open fields to get to this place.

He silently thanked Jack Wade for pointing it out to

him on their long drive around on the day of his arrival in St Petersburg. Later, when the gangster arms dealer Zukovsky had mentioned the rumours that Janus travelled in style on an armoured train, Bond had known immediately where that train was likely to be kept: here, the once Number One Strategic (Rail) Weapons Depot. The first real proof of what this place had been was in the number of long, strengthened, flatbed trucks, which had been the main transporter vehicles for NATO-coded Scapegoats, Savage, Sego and Scrooge nuclear weapons – the ICBMs and tactical nukes which were taken by rail to sites and silos, or even intended to be launched from these very trucks.

The track itself appeared to be in good order, as did the one train standing in the depot. A large diesel-powered, heavily armoured engine was set to pull three carriages. Each seemed identical and was also armoured. The engine was already running at idle, and from its square nose a single, long, telescopic, steel buffer projected. At its foremost end was a circular plate, almost the same circumference as the front plate of the engine itself.

The buffer, he thought, would be enough to deter anyone attempting to get in the way of the engine. It would also act as an effective shock absorber should such an engine be pulling a nuclear load.

He was thinking that the entire train had been well refurbished, when the car swept out of an underground tunnel to screech to a halt beside the platform.

He would make sure they were on board before he moved off, for it should take him no longer than ten minutes to travel below the ridge of the cutting, then down to the point where he planned once again to come face to face with Janus.

*   *   *

Ourumov dragged the girl from the back and turned to the driver.

Natalya cowered behind the general.

'Shall I wait, sir?' the driver asked.

Ourumov nodded. 'If you would. Wait for ever, please.' He shot him. Twice in the stomach and then once through the head – the *coup de grâce* – as he lay dying on the ground.

Revolted, Natalya turned away, then jumped backwards in surprise, for Xenia Onatopp had silently come from the train and was standing directly behind her.

'Welcome, Natalya.' She gave a wolfish smile and wiggled her hips slightly. She wore a skin-tight one-piece black jump suit and highly polished calf-length boots. An Uzi hung from her shoulder. 'Arkady.' She leaned forward and kissed the general. 'It's wonderful to see you both here safely. Janus is going to be so pleased.'

'Not with what I've got to tell him.' Ourumov sounded surly.

'Never mind. Such romps we'll all have, and think of that wonderful sun. Come, little one.' She looked at Natalya as though she could eat her.

As they half pulled Natalya towards the train, Ourumov seemed to throw off his surliness. 'Ah, I shall enjoy a little sunshine after the winter we've had.' Then he laughed – an unpleasant cackle. 'Natalya, you'll be fine sport. I know you'll have fun. Xenia is an extraordinary woman. She likes anything with legs. Rather exotic tastes, our Xenia has, yes.'

Natalya found, on boarding the train, that it did not smell as she expected a train to smell – even a diesel. There was none of that mixture of sweat, oil and grease she was used to. Instead she smelled flowers, roses, the air was sweet with them.

When they took her into Alec Trevelyan's carriage she gasped at the opulence. She had seen photographs of the Czar Nicholas's train, with its rich hangings, chandeliers, beautiful upholstered seats, fine mahogany panelling and polished tables. This seemed to be a replica.

Trevelyan sat at one of the tables which was laid out for breakfast. That was the other thing Natalya could smell – fresh and rich coffee. The china on the breakfast table was like nothing she had ever seen: each cup, saucer and plate was ringed with a thin gold band sandwiched between two royal blue bands, while each piece also contained what seemed to be a royal crest: a blue shield on which there were two gold profiles, as though a face had been split in two. Like the man sitting drinking his coffee: the right side clear and unharmed, his left side scarred and terrible, with the eye socket pulled down out of alignment, and the mouth frozen at the corner. Between eye and mouth, the ruined flesh seemed like the skin of a reptile.

As he stared at her, Natalya felt movement. The train was beginning its journey, swaying slightly and gathering speed.

The man with the disfigured face, whom she took to be Janus, glanced at Ourumov and then his eyes switched to Natalya, looking her slowly up and down so that she felt he was mentally undressing her. It was a humiliating experience, and for the time this went on, she felt as though this strange man really had the power to see her body through her clothes. She would not look him in the eye, turning away her head in embarrassment.

Finally he spoke to Ourumov, 'Either you've brought me this perfect gift for our long journey, General, or you've made me a very unhappy man.'

Ourumov gave a shrug, as though nothing mattered

either way. 'That idiot Mishkin got to them before I could.'

'What you're really trying to tell me is that Bond is alive.'

Another shrug. 'He escaped.'

The scaly and askew side of his face seemed to give a twitch. 'Good for Bond,' he murmured. Then lifting his head, 'But bad for you, General.'

Xenia gave an unpleasant croaking laugh. 'I told you that if I couldn't get this man Bond, then you wouldn't have any success either,' taunting the general.

Trevelyan shook his head. 'Bond has as many spare lives as a cat. Now, bring her over here.' He motioned towards Natalya.

Ourumov put a hand on her shoulder and propelled her roughly towards Janus/Trevelyan, thrusting her down in the padded chair next to him.

'Just sit quietly, and be a good girl.' Trevelyan spoke softly, and she noticed that he had a very similar accent to that of Bond. When he leaned forward, his face close to hers, she wanted to pull away. It was not the disfigurement as much as something about the man's personality. Not just unpleasant, but bordering on evil.

'You like my friend, James?' he asked.

She gave a noncommittal nod, just the slightest movement of her head.

'Well, my dear, James and I shared everything at one time.' When he smiled it was only with the right side of his mouth, and the left eye seemed to close, its reptilian eyelid sliding down very slowly. The eye reminded her of a lizard or a chameleon.

As he came even closer she smelled a cologne and coffee, but something else. For a second she could not place it, then realised that it was the smell of burning flesh, and she did not know whether she was imagining this or not. Someone had once told her that when it rained in Berlin you could still smell the burning of that city: the hint of how it had smelled after countless bombings and the final bombardment that had taken place fifty years ago, during the war.

He must have sensed that she was trying to pull back from him. 'We shared absolutely everything, and you must understand that to the victor go the spoils. You can make your life very pleasant. You can even live in luxury for some time. Eventually you will come to like me very much.' His lips brushed her neck, then he moved a hand, turning her face, lowering his lips to her mouth.

She allowed him to get close, then, like an unpredictable animal, she opened her mouth and snapped at his lip. She felt her teeth going in and saw, as he pulled back with a little cry of annoyance, that she had broken the skin. Blood was running from the lip.

She did not see his hand come up to slap her hard, only feeling the sting of sudden pain as her head was pushed sideways. 'You bastard,' she spat at him.

'I like a spirited woman.' He gave his warped smile again. 'A woman with your kind of liveliness is much more fun than some docile bitch who just lies there like a pillow. I shall enjoy breaking you, Natalya Fyodorovna.'

Her eyes opened wide with surprise. 'How do you know my name?'

The smile again, this time broader and, therefore, more sinister. 'You'd be surprised at what I know. . . .'

As he moved towards her again, there was a shrill, piercing alarm which seemed to surround them like some tangible envelope. She also saw red lights blinking on the roof of the carriage.

He pushed her roughly out of the way and spoke to

Ourumov, telling him to stay and watch her. Then he was running fast towards the next carriage, Xenia, with the little Uzi at the ready, following him.

In the short time Bond had available, he had chosen the best possible point for his ambush on a mile length of straight railway track leading into a short tunnel.

The tank had nearly up-ended itself as he went down the embankment close to the place he wanted to use, but finally he manoeuvred the machine into position, lining up its tracks on the rails so that it faced in the direction from which Trevelyan's armoured train would come.

He opened the hatch, climbed into the gunner's seat and examined the shells in their racks. The T55 carried three types of shell for the 100mm gun: Smoke, High Explosive and Armour Piercing. Bond did not have to think twice. The gun was easy enough to load, and with the engine at idle, he could swing the turret and depress the barrel so that it was pointing directly at where the train would appear.

It was yet another calculated risk, for Trevelyan might easily play things safe and back up as soon as the tank was spotted: a move that could quickly take the train out of range. He was also gambling on Natalya being held somewhere in the rear of the carriages. He would only have one chance, one shell to take out the engine, and almost as soon as he had depressed the firing button it would be necessary for him to be up and away through the hatch.

Strangely, the only thing worrying him was the very small amount of ammunition in the machine pistol. He thought it would now be about six rounds, which were not enough to take out Trevelyan and his lieutenants.

Sufficient unto the day is the evil thereof. The Biblical

quote came back to him together with familiar scents from the past, the smell of chalk and other boys; of damp grey flannel and the harsh penalties for flouting rules.

Pressing his eye to the forward sight, he saw that the train had already begun to move swiftly into view.

Trevelyan and Xenia had moved forward into the Communications Carriage, filled with state-of-the-art computers and communications electronics which would keep them in touch with the entire world if need be.

At the far end a monitor linked them with a camera set high at the front of the engine. When he saw the tank, stationary on the rails ahead as they closed fast, Trevelyan uncharacteristically sighed, then made a noise which mingled anger with a hint of admiration. 'Only James Bond,' he muttered.

'He'll derail us. We must stop!' Xenia showed some panic in her usually calm and cool manner.

'No!' from Trevelyan.

'What do we do?' The question came from up front in the train's cabin, and it was obvious that the driver and his engineer were already slowing slightly. The brakes had started to pump.

'Stop that.' Trevelyan had snatched at a small microphone attached to the wall. 'Go for him. Full speed. Ram him.'

'But . . .' came the driver's voice.

'Ram him, damn you. You have that damned great battering ram up front. Now's the time to use it.'

The words and confidence were easy, but the situation had certain very dangerous drawbacks. Trevelyan was experienced enough to know what was going on. He too was a gambler. Whatever happened now, he thought, the train would be wrecked. Well, that was OK for he would have no difficulty finding an alternative method of transport. It was an irritation, a minor setback, but they would still get to their destination.

He looked up at the monitor and braced himself in his seat. Opposite him, Xenia was also straining backwards in her seat, the Uzi held across her lap and her legs straight. Above them the monitor showed that they were rushing towards the tank at high speed. About six hundred yards to go and closing very fast.

At around two hundred yards Trevelyan began to feel the first nip of fear in the back of his mind. Then there was a flash, followed by a great heaving as though the carriage were being shaken by an earthquake.

Bond had banged down on the firing button. The turret bucked under the recoil and the shell penetrated the front of the engine, exploding with a great sheet of flame which seemed to reach out as though trying to devour the tank.

He pulled himself up through the hatch, leaped to the left and rolled away towards the bank, almost at the moment the train's engine hit the tank, the long telescopic buffer buckling under the impact.

Bond dug himself into the earth as the forward momentum of the engine pushed the tank, now on fire, back into the tunnel.

Then came the second explosion: a thunderous clap of noise and a searing heat which even Bond felt, lying on the ground a good distance away. He raised his head and saw the wide plume of flame and smoke coming from inside the tunnel, the mixture of fuel and explosives rising into the air, as though drawing a deadly question mark.

By the time that happened, Bond was on his feet, the machine pistol in his hand, running full tilt towards the carriages, looking for the easiest way in.

He saw the steps at the door linking the last and middle

carriages and threw himself towards them, his hand touching hot metal, his heart set on finishing the business with Trevelyan once and for all.

In the Communications Carriage, both Xenia and Trevelyan had been thrown to the ground; equipment had detached itself from walls and desk tops. Xenia's Uzi had skittered back along the aisle and, worst of all, they were plunged into darkness.

'Emergency generator!' Trevelyan shouted, and Xenia stumbled forward, feeling her way to the large wall switch which would give them power now that the engine had exploded taking with it their normal source of electricity.

She pulled down on the switch and, as the lights came back on –

'Just stay absolutely still.' The voice came from behind them.

Trevelyan, half sprawled across a table, did not even bother to look around. 'James, why can't you just die like any other normal person?' he asked.

15

Steel-Plated Coffin

Alec Trevelyan's almost casual manner was meant to either anger Bond, or put him off guard. It did neither. He remembered the many tricks Trevelyan always had up his sleeve back in the old days, when they were cold warriors together. Bond particularly recalled a seminar at which Trevelyan spoke of the need for the man in the field never to show any true emotion, and always to appear utterly uncaring about anything if caught out.

Much had obviously happened to Alec in the years between, but he had almost certainly never lost his old way of working. If he appeared relaxed after what had happened in the last few minutes, then he obviously had some surprises in store, so it was necessary to treat him with considerable care.

Both Trevelyan and Xenia stood with their backs towards Bond and a little too close to various switches and buttons that probably meant they could shut off the light, or open doors to go into the carriage forward of the middle one in which they stood.

The train's engine had uncoupled itself from the three

cars as it plunged into the tunnel, and he was uncertain whether Natalya was being held in the carriage forward of where his prisoners stood, or the one behind. He also needed a new weapon and, as the two prisoners remained facing away from him, Bond's eyes flicked to and fro, finally alighting on a small hand gun – a Beretta, he thought – lying on one of the computer tables which had not suffered damage in the collision and blast.

He stepped to one side, picked it up and cocked the mechanism. The weight of the gun told him it had a full magazine, so working the slide ensured a round was chambered.

'Turn around, with your hands on your head,' he ordered. 'Both of you. Now!'

As they obeyed, he saw Xenia's eyes move towards her Uzi which lay on the floor about three feet away from her.

'Kick that towards me, please, Xenia. We don't want any accidents. Now, both of you stand well clear of that door.' The Uzi slid towards him, and while his pistol did not waver, Bond caught the machine gun with the side of his foot, sending it under the seats to his right.

Trevelyan gave a mocking laugh. 'James, you've always been lucky. But by the same token you've always been foolhardy. You perform well under pressure but you never think ahead. You haven't a chance here. You have no backup and no escape route. You're stuck here with us as your hostages. A poet once wrote, "The glass is falling hour by hour. . . ."'

Bond continued the quote, ' "The glass will fall for ever. But if you break the bloody glass, you won't hold up the weather." Yes, I know, Alec, and I'm quite aware that you probably have some earth-shattering plan already running. . . .'

'Earth-shattering is good. Very good, James. And, no!

No, you cannot stop it now. Unless you can find the source and remove that bad boy Boris within a couple of days, you're done for, old son. Buggered and bitched. I am the only person who might possibly change the circumstances, but that's pretty unlikely now. And I hold the trump card here. I hold the bargaining chip, so to speak.'

'Oh?'

'I have the beautiful Natalya.'

'So?'

'What do you mean, James, so?'

'Why should Natalya be a bargaining chip?'

'Come on, James. I know you very well.'

'You do? Where is she, then? Where is she if she's such an asset?'

'I can get her for you, only you'll have to let me use the microphone.' His head gestured to where the mike was hanging, attached to a wall mounting. 'I just need your permission to. . . .'

'Don't do anything stupid, Alec. I really don't want to kill you. I want to take you home.'

'Oh, yes. Home. By which I presume you mean England, home and beauty?'

'No, I mean England, home and justice.'

Trevelyan gestured towards the microphone once more and Bond nodded, not moving his eyes, but keeping the pistol halfway between Trevelyan and Xenia.

'Ourumov! Bring her in here.' Trevelyan spoke into the mike and then returned it to the wall bracket. 'A lovely girl. Tastes like . . . Well, I think she tastes like strawberries. You always had a yen for strawberry-flavoured girls, James.'

'I wouldn't know what she tastes like.'

'A pity. I *know*.' He was a clever actor, Bond thought. In that simple line the man had conjured up a picture of countless nights spent in the arms of Natalya, of every possible kind of fleshly lust studied and practised with her.

The door behind him slid open and Natalya came hobbling in. General Ourumov had one arm around her throat, pulling her back towards him, while his other hand held a pistol to her head.

Trevelyan laughed. Not simply a laugh of pleasure or mockery, Bond considered. That was the laugh of a madman. 'Here we go again, James.' Even Bond thought that the man was a shade too cool. There had to be something. Trevelyan was far too relaxed for comfort.

'The good old Mexican standoff, James. Also, if you think about it, we're back to where we started. You've got one choice. Either your little friend with Ourumov, or the mission to see what I have and where it's hidden.'

Keeping the Beretta trained on the other two, Bond turned his head slightly so that Ourumov would know he was being spoken to. 'General, tell me, what's this Cossack promised you?'

Out of the corner of his eye he could see a twitch of uncertainty cross Ourumov's face.

'Details. Details,' Trevelyan murmured.

'You know, surely, General Ourumov? You know he's a Lienz Cossack?'

'Long ago and far away. Like a playwright once said about fornication. "That was in another country, and besides, the wench is dead."'

'This is true?' Ourumov sounded shaken.

'About another country?' Trevelyan gave a high, one breath, laugh.

'It's true, Ourumov. He's a Lienz Cossack and you know they all have long memories of the purges. He has no love for you or your kind. He'll betray you. Just like he's betrayed everyone else.'

166

'This *is* true?' Ourumov asked again, and was cut off by Trevelyan.

'What's true is that in forty-eight to seventy-two hours you and I will have more money and more power than God. By then, Mr Bond here will have only a small memorial service, and I doubt if there'll be many people left to attend it. Should there be, it'll be Moneypenny weeping and a dozen or so restaurateurs worrying about their bank balances. But a lot of people'll be worrying about their bank balances by then.' He paused for it to sink in. 'So what's it to be, James? Two targets. Time for one shot. Which way will you jump? The girl or the mission?'

Bond shrugged. 'Kill the girl if you like. She means nothing to me.'

Natalya let out a little moan which seemed to come from deep inside her.

'See you in hell, James.' He nodded his command to Ourumov to kill the girl, but the general was off his guard now and Natalya sucked in that extra adrenalin. She broke free and kneed him in the groin, diving away from him as she did so, leaving Bond a clear shot.

The pistol barked, sounding like a cannon in the enclosed space of the carriage and, as though in slow motion, the top of Ourumov's head disappeared in a fine red mist.

Bond ducked sideways, threw himself down near Natalya and came up shooting. His first two rounds went high, to the left. By the time he resighted, the door at the far end was open and Xenia, followed by Trevelyan, was through the gap. Two more shots splintered the woodwork, but they were out and away. As he reached the door, he heard the sound of bolts being thrown. Almost at the same time great thick armoured shields came clanging down over the windows.

'We're in an armour-plated coffin,' Bond said quietly.

'Yes, I'm fine, thank you, James. Good of you to ask.'

'I'm sorry, but. . . .'

The one big computer, on the desk from where Bond had snatched the Beretta, suddenly beeped, and Natalya turned her head. Took one look and shouted, 'Boris?'

'Where?'

'Somewhere out there.' She pushed him to one side and swung into the chair, her hands on the keyboard, rattling away.

'Natalya, what in hell're you doing?'

'James, let me get on with it. Somewhere out there, in the real world, Boris is sitting at a computer. That's where you'd expect him to be. He's only alive when he's at a computer. He could be anywhere – Timbukthree. . . .'

'Timbuktu.'

'Two. Right. Now, this is his programme. He's backing up all his files and he's reachable. If I can send a spike down the line, I could trace exactly where he is. Would that help?'

'Just a lot.'

'Good, then let me do it.' She growled at him, 'Well, don't just stand there, man, get us out of here.'

'Yes, sir. Certainly, sir. Three bags full, sir.' He turned his attention to the floor, and removing a large Swiss Army knife from its hiding place in the waistband of his slacks, he began to cut away a wide section of the carpeting.

Outside, Trevelyan and Xenia had jumped from the train. 'I only hope to God that it wasn't damaged in the blast.' He sounded concerned now. 'If it was then we can say goodbye to everything.'

They stood back from the forward coach, the front of

168

which looked a little charred and burned from the explosion.

Taking what looked like a small TV remote controller from his pocket, Trevelyan aimed it at the carriage and pressed.

There was a rumbling and the four sides fell away on hinges to reveal a sleek, black, little helicopter.

'We did it!' Xenia shouted as she and Trevelyan ran up one of the long, oblong sides and onto the flatbed truck, moving as a team, unclipping padded metal restraining locks from around the machine.

Seconds later, Trevelyan ducked underneath the middle carriage and heard the sounds of Bond at work. His hand slid up to a black box towards the front of the carriage, opened it and punched in some numbers.

By the time he reappeared, Xenia had the engine running and the rotors turning. A few seconds later the helicopter lifted off, with Trevelyan at the controls. He flew in a wide arc and then hovered over the centre carriage, speaking quickly into a sound system which magnified his voice.

Natalya was typing furiously, the read-out on her monitor flashing and changing:

C:>   CD SPIKE

C:>SPIKE

C:>SEND SPIKE ENTER

She slammed a forefinger onto the enter key and the prompt came up:

C:>SPIKE SENT

She gave a wild war whoop. 'Got him, I hope.' Then they both heard the disembodied voice of Janus, Alec Trevelyan, coming from above.

'Good luck with the floor, James. I set the timers for

three minutes. The same three minutes you gave me back near Archangel. It was the least I could do for an old friend.'

An intermittent beeping sounded from below them, and red lights began to flash above each door in the carriage.

'What does that mean?' Natalya sounded anxious.

'It means we've got exactly sixty seconds to get out.'

'Oh.' She went back to the keyboard, typing even faster.

Bond had the carpet stripped back to expose the metal floor. He pulled his watch from his wrist, turned the bezel so that two marks were aligned, then he pressed one of the buttons flanking the main stem. A thin, bright laser beam hissed out of the side. Lowering it, he began to slice through the steel, tearing it away and making a wide circle. The watch was one of the most useful things Q had ever provided him with.

Natalya had typed in a further command: C:> FOLLOW SPIKE TRACE. Her screen dissolved and a map appeared in its place. She followed the red line that traced itself across the graphics of the world, talking as it went. 'He's not in Russia, Germany, Paris, Madrid, Rome, London.' Her voice became faster and faster as the line followed Boris, and the confusing route he had taken. 'New York, Washington, Miami, Key West. . . .'

'Twenty seconds . . .' Bond shouted.

'Cuba. James, he's in Cuba. . . .'

Bond thumped the centre of the laser tracing and a circular sheet of steel dropped to the ground below the carriage. 'Fifteen,' he yelled.

'Havana! Got him . . . No. No, he's out of there. To the north but still in Cuba. . . .'

'Near enough!' He yanked at the back of her shirt, dragged her from the chair and dropped her through the hole, following her with about five seconds to go.

They crawled out very quickly and he flung her down, covering her body, just as the three carriages went up with a roar, engulfed in flame.

Natalya sprinted up to the far side of the bank, Bond went after her, again ending up shielding her.

She smiled up at him. 'Wow! Was it good for you?'

'A shade too close for comfort.'

'I don't get it, James. What is it with you? Do you destroy every vehicle you get into?'

'It does seem to have become a kind of operating procedure.'

'Well, I think I should make the arrangements for our trip to Cuba.'

'Our trip?'

'You don't think I'm going to leave you to finish this on your own, do you? Anyway, do *you* know how to dismantle *Mischa*?'

'Actually, now that you mention it, no. We may need some help.'

'Can you find it?'

'Oh, I think so.'

'Good. Now, James, are there any other operating procedures I should know about?'

'Thousands.' He smiled at her, his lips drifting down towards her mouth. 'Don't worry, though. I only pay them lip service.'

'I can't think of a better way,' said Natalya Simonova as she lifted her face, and then her body, to his.

16

Interlude

There were a lot of problems and the first, which should have been the easiest, proved to be the most difficult. They were on foot, some six or seven miles from the centre of St Petersburg. In these days of the new Russian democracy, it was not always a good idea to be without transport. Bond also needed a telephone to accomplish the most essential hurdle: getting in touch with Jack Wade, his only backup.

They walked for several miles, happily unmolested but for a beggar who insisted on singing for them in a high-pitched tuneless voice. From what Bond could make out, the words had something to do with, 'Oh, my suffering brothers'. As the man sang, so he thought he heard the sound of a bell in the distance. The bell was also tuneless, like the snapping of a wire.

Against his better judgement, he gave the man a fortune – five dollars – and asked Natalya what it was all about.

'Oh, it's an old revolutionary song, from before the Bolshevik days,' she told him.

Finally, they reached a grubby little restaurant where

the proprietor agreed to let them use his telephone for a price, and on condition that they had breakfast, paying for that as well.

Bond dialled the number Jack Wade had given him and got Wade's voice telling him to leave a message and have a nice day. He told the CIA man where they were, that they needed transport and a lot of other favours.

The coffee was surprisingly good, and they also ate some smoked herring with black bread.

They had just finished eating when two police cars squealed to a halt outside.

'The game's up,' Bond whispered. 'We're in trouble.'

The proprietor had other ideas. He was obviously a man who had some kind of grudge against authority in any shape or form. He came out from behind the counter like a greyhound unleashed.

Whispering in rapid Russian, the man quickly shepherded them through the back room, up a short flight of stairs and into a large cupboard which contained cans and boxes of prepackaged food and cooking oil. Black Market, Bond thought, then the proprietor put his finger to his lips and closed the door, leaving them in pitch dark.

Natalya's hand came up to his face, her fingers exploring eyes, nose, mouth and chin.

Bond drew her close, leaned over and found her mouth with his. At first she did not respond as his lips caressed hers, then, like throwing a switch, he felt her body thrust against his, and she opened her mouth.

From below came the sound of argument, then laughter. After around twenty minutes they heard the proprietor's footsteps on the stairs. He grinned as he opened the door.

'Some fools have been tampering with weapons and railway equipment.' He gave them a gap-toothed grin.

'The Police and Security Organs are looking for a man and a woman. I try not to bother with these people so I told them I'd had no customers this morning. Good? Yes?'

'Very good.' Bond gave him money which made him even happier.

About half an hour later, Wade turned up, still in the battered old Moscovich, flashing a radiant smile. In the car, heading back to the hotel, Bond gave him a shopping list which included tickets on the first available plane to the United States, a valid passport with the right visas for Natalya, and some changes of clothes for the girl.

'This ain't gonna be the easiest job in the world.' Wade's voice was languid, as though it did not matter one way or the other to him. 'On the other hand it ain't gonna be impossible.'

He suddenly swung the car across the road, hanging a right into narrow country lane.

'There's no room to pass anything.' Bond sounded irritable. 'Why this farm track, Jack?'

'Because of the road blocks and their other games, James.'

'Road blocks?' Natalya was getting edgy.

'Yeah, like cars, saw horses, cops, KGB. . . .'

'KGB doesn't exist any more,' Natalya bridled.

'Sure, that's why everyone still calls it that, or the old name Cheka. Interchangeable, babe. If *you* don't know that, someone's been putting happy dust into your breakfast cereal. I don't know a single Russian who calls KGB anything else but KGB – yesterday, today, forever, like the ads for that musical, *Kittens*.'

'*Cats*,' Bond corrected.

'Whatever. Anyways, the outskirts are crawling with people looking to do dangerous things to you. I did a quick checkup, and for some reason they don't seem to know where you've been staying, James. They not take your passport at the hotel?'

'No. The booking was what in the trade is known as clandestine.'

'Our trade as well. Gee, we use the same words; and they say Britain and America are two countries separated by the same language.'

After a pause, Bond asked if he understood Wade correctly. 'What you're saying is that nobody's got the hotel under surveillance?'

'Clean as the proverbial whistle. No pack drill, no names, James.'

'So what else?'

'We can sneak around these lanes and the backstreets. Once we're in central St Petersburg there doesn't seem to be a general alert. These people're funny. I guess they figure that nobody would be stupid enough to come right into town.'

'And?'

'And that's the good news. The bad news is that the train stations and airports are crawling with the secret squirrels. You're both gonna need new passports, and I fear we're forced to use some old-fashioned remedy, like disguise.'

Bond hated disguises; never felt happy wearing them; found it difficult to take on some new role. He made a lame protest, saying he wasn't going to wear fancy dress, not for anybody.

'Don't worry, James. We'll be subtle. We won't put you in drag. Just age you a bit, and Natalya can be aged down. It'll be cool. Don't worry.'

At the hotel, nobody challenged them. They showered and then waited, wondering if Jack Wade would really come up with the goods.

He was, in fact, surprisingly fast, and at around seven o'clock he arrived at their room with a case full of what he insisted on calling 'goodies' plus a pair of flight bags.

There was an American passport for Bond, complete with a new face which sported large heavy spectacles, grey hair and a chubbier face. These last changes were simple: a grey rinse for the hair, and foam pads to go into his cheeks.

'Don't try and drink anything while you're wearing those in your mouth, James. They tend to suck up liquids so you spray everyone.'

'I read that in an upmarket espionage novel some-where.' He went into the bathroom, rinsed his hair with the special preparation, put the glasses on, and slid the pads into his cheeks. The change in his appearance was really quite remarkable, and he emerged into the sitting room to find Wade with a young schoolgirl he did not recognise.

'She's meant to be around fifteen. Brit passport with the correct visa, and the school uniform really does exist.' Wade gave her an almost lecherous look. 'You have real passports for the onward journey.' He dumped a pair of old style British passports on the table. 'You all happy now?'

'I like the – what do you call it? Gymslip?' Natalya lowered her eyes, as though embarrassed.

'That's correct.' Bond looked her up and down, the white knee socks did his libido a power of good.

'What I don't like is the underwear. Thick, dark blue and feels like serge.'

Bond smiled. 'Standard uniform issue at British girls' schools.'

'Only for the flight.' Wade put on an innocent look. 'There'll be a bag of really nice clothes for both of you when you get to where you're going. I took the liberty of working out your sizes. In the meantime you've got a flight bag each with one or two things that should help.'

They separated at the airport where the security forces were all over the place. Bond presented himself at immigration as a crusty, no-nonsense, slightly eccentric ex-military type abroad. He found it worked wonders when he threatened to report an over zealous official.

On the air side his heart skipped a few beats when he saw two large female security officers take Natalya into a curtained off area. Later, she told him it was the worst moment of her life. 'I think there was something funny about them. Very aggressive, until I gave them some dollars. They stopped mauling me after that.'

The flight took them to Paris where they had enough time to change back into near normal representations of themselves, and on the flight to Miami sat with each other. There were no awkward questions on arrival, and they just made the connection to Puerto Rico where they were met by a young man who had CIA written all over him, and who took them through immigration and customs with a minimum amount of bother. The young man, who was stocky, built like a fireplug and answered to the name Mac, had their new luggage with him. He appeared to be very taken with Natalya.

He drove them to a luxurious beach house in an equally luxurious BMW which he said was for their use while they were on the island.

The following afternoon found them on the road, exploring the island, away from all the tourist haunts in San Juan.

'You don't know what this means to me.' Natalya's hair was ruffled by the warm breeze as they negotiated empty roads far off the normal guided tour routes. 'You know,

James, all my life I wanted to come to the Caribbean. I even had a picture of one of the islands – St Thomas, I think – at my work-station at Severnaya. Dreamed about it since I was a small girl, and I can't believe I'm here.'

'I'm glad we had the opportunity of making your dreams come true.' Bond smiled at her. 'I just hope we don't end up in a nightmare.'

She ignored the last remark, sighed, lying her head on his shoulder. 'Here we are, on a beautiful island and not another human being in sight.'

As she said it, so a loud beeping came from the radio panel.

'That could be our wake-up call.' Bond stabbed at one of the pre-set buttons on the radio and a panel dropped down to reveal a small radar screen with one green blip showing each time the sweep line circled the display. 'It appears that we have company.' Bond's brow wrinkled, and from far away, over the noise of the car, they both became aware of the sound of an approaching aircraft.

He saw it in the rear-view mirror, and Natalya turned to look back, giving a little squeak of surprise, ducking low down in her seat just as a neat little Piper Archer passed low over their heads, flaps fully extended, so that it could land on the road in front of them.

'You were saying?' Bond's face showed nothing, but his hand slipped inside his blazer and he placed an automatic pistol on the console between them.

The Archer taxied on up the road and finally turned left, going through a gap in the trees and coming to a stop in an empty field.

'Do you work at attracting trouble with anything that moves?' Natalya looked puzzled.

'It's my natural charm.' He still showed no emotion. 'That, combined with a weakness for causing mayhem and often a lot of violence.' He braked and turned into the field, drawing up close to the Archer which had the name *Lord Geoff I* stencilled on its nose.

As they came to a halt, Jack Wade clambered down from the passenger seat, carrying a small briefcase.

'Jimbo!' he greeted Bond.

'I told you never to call me that. And while we're at it, what're you doing here?'

'You wanted the job of finishing off Janus, and I bring tidings from your boss. She says you're to go ahead. Tomorrow, in fact. Oh, this is a present from what's his name – N? R? A?'

'Q.'

'That's the one.' He handed over the briefcase, sniffing at the air. 'Ah, Banyan trees.' He paused and then, 'Incidentally, I'm not here, capish? The Agency has absolutely nothing to do with this. No knowledge. Nothing to do with your insertion into Cuba. OK?'

Bond nodded.

'I borrowed this little baby from a friend of mine in the Drugs Enforcement Agency. It'll be waiting for you, all ready to go, at the private aircraft parking at San Juan Dominicci, first light tomorrow morning.'

'We'll be there.' Dominicci is San Juan's domestic airport at which shuttles depart and arrive all day from the outlying towns on the island.

'Just climb aboard and give your call sign, Smiley One. Now . . .' He walked them to the door of the aircraft and took some papers from the seat. 'We've covered you in every possible way. Coast Guard, Federal Aviation Authority and Southern Military Command are all in the loop, and when I said first light, I meant it. You'll be cleared at 06.00.'

He handed over a large manila envelope. 'This is the

latest Satint from the Puzzle Palace. They say you should be OK as long as you stay at under six hundred feet.'

Natalya's hand shot forward, plucking the envelope from Bond's hand. 'Five hundred feet,' she smiled like a nice, well brought-up Russian girl.

'Who is this?' Wade cocked his head on one side, looking quizzically at Natalya, as though he had never met her.

'I should've introduced you. You brought her clothes in Petersburg, remember?'

'Ah, yes, I remember it well. Natalya Simonova.'

Natalya looked from under half closed lids as she ripped the envelope open and began studying its contents of maps and satellite photographs. 'I have been promoted. Now I'm a deputy sheriff of Mr Bond's posse.' She gave Wade an enormous smile. 'You have a very weird taste in certain more intimate garments, Mr Wade.'

'Oh, yes. I hope they were the right size.'

'Perfect.' Bond looked at them with innocence written all over his face.

'This Russian girl here? You check her out?'

'From head to toe, Jacko.'

'Please don't call me . . .' He stopped as he saw Natalya scrutinising the satellite maps. Leaning over her, he pointed. 'You'll be looking for a satellite dish the size of a football field, I presume? Well, it just doesn't exist. Nobody can light up a cigar in Cuba without the boys at the National Security Agency knowing about it. It just is *not* there.'

Natalya gave him a cheeky smile. 'Mr Wade, I know it's there. It's an exact replica of the one at Severnaya.'

Bond interrupted them. 'What if we need backup, Jack?'

'There's a transmitter in the plane.' He indicated an

area among the instruments in front of the pilot, who remained silent and did not even look in their direction. 'It'll send a warning if the plane comes unstuck. Either way, if you're in trouble, just squawk and I'll send in the Marines.'

For the first time, the pilot leaned down, gesturing to Wade to hurry up. 'My chauffeur's getting anxious.' He clapped Bond on the shoulder and kissed Natalya on the cheek. 'Just hang a right at the end of the runway. It's only a short ride to Cuba from there. Good luck. I'll pick up the BMW at Dominicci in the morning.'

'Well, try not to touch any odd buttons in it.'

'I was just goin' to bomb around in it for a while.'

'Exactly.'

'James, you can take Janus out. I have all the faith in the world, because you know all that guy's moves.'

'The problem is that he knows all of mine as well. We worked together for a very long time.'

'You'll still take him, Jimbo.' Wade leaped out of the range of Bond's closed fist and climbed back into the Piper Archer, which slowly began to taxi away.

That night, Bond checked out Q's briefcase in the privacy of the beach house. It contained a new watch and six small magnetic charges which could be controlled by it. He packed them away among the kit he would be wearing the next morning.

Outside, on the beach he sat down near the surf, wrapped in thought as he was lulled by the noise of the sea. He thought of all the years he had spent living in secret yet enjoying everything that his hedonistic life had to offer.

What had he become, he asked himself. Was he just a killing machine? Did his superiors let him get away with all kinds of excesses both on and off missions because they understood the kind of strain his work produced? He knew that some people turned a blind eye to certain aspects of his way of life, just as he knew that they paid him more than most of the regular officers of the Secret Intelligence Service.

He went back over so much of his life that he wondered if he were getting maudlin about things, like a drunk ready to cry into his beer. He really had to snap out of this, it was not doing any good.

Natalya came barefoot across the sand, turning her face towards the sea breeze as she stood close to him. Presently she reached down and tousled his hair, but he did not move, and even seemed unaware of her presence until she spoke, squatting on the sand next to him.

'Janus was your friend, wasn't he?' he asked.

'Several lifetimes ago, yes.'

'And now he is your enemy. So tomorrow you'll go and kill him. It's that simple, yes?'

'Yes.'

She drew in breath through her nostrils. The sound made him look at her and he saw the anger in her eyes. 'No, James. No, it's not that easy.'

She tried to get up from the sand, but he grabbed her arm and drew her back to him.

'I hate you,' she spat like an angry cat. 'I hate you. I hate all of you. Your kind've caused so much grief all over the world, with your guns and your instruments of death.'

She began hitting at him, pummelling his chest. He enveloped her in his arms, holding her tightly as her fighting became less violent and she began to cry softly. 'So many of my friends,' she sobbed. 'My friends, members of my family. So many have died because of people like you.'

'There have to be people like me.' He hugged her close. 'I do a necessary job. If I didn't do it, someone else would. I simply have to level things off so that one day there will be some true kind of peace in the world.'

After a while, her sobbing stopped, and he helped her to her feet. Together they walked back to the house.

Inside, the air was cooled by two overhead fans; the lights were turned down to a pleasant dusk-like glow; the stereo was playing the late Miles Davis' evergreen 'Sketches of Spain': the soft lush sound of the waves breaking on the beach outside counterpointing the music.

They stood close together, all senses merging, hands touching, their nostrils gathering up the pleasant smell of island flowers combining with faintly aromatic scents of the dish, which Bond had set to cook slowly in the kitchen.

When he kissed her, he tasted the aftermath of sweet fruit. When she kissed him back, her tongue sliced into his mouth, caressing the inside of his cheeks, coming away with the slight tang of the champagne he had sipped less than an hour before.

He took her by the hand and she followed him, eyes downcast as though she were completely innocent of men, which would have been a lie. In front of the bed they slowly undressed each other. She wore no bra under her T-shirt, and only the flimsiest garment was revealed as her skirt dropped to the floor.

She gave a little giggle and whispered, 'More romantic than the schoolgirl pants, eh?'

'And softer on the skin.' The little white froth of nylon fell to the floor and she stepped forward, yanking at his belt and stripping the thin lightweight pants from his legs. In the distance, she seemed to hear her mother, flustered, *Natalya have you no shame* when, years ago, she had caught her with a local boy.

She allowed him to turn her and lift her onto the bed. He slid quietly on top of her, taking his weight on his forearms, and Natalya suddenly sucked in air as her hands enfolded him. Embracing him with her fingers, she pulled him to her lips and kissed him, then pushed him back so that his manhood lay across her belly.

She felt his hands slide under her buttocks, pressing, stroking and kneading them as he bent his mouth to kiss first one breast and then the other. Her hands guided him down and he slid into her, thick and long so that she lifted her buttocks in his hands and let out a sharp breath of pleasure.

They had become one person, locked and moving slowly through the wonder of that great pleasure only woman can give to man, and man to woman.

Both of them had dreamed of nights like this from the first moment of meeting though neither would have ever admitted it, as they found the rhythm, lost it, then discovered a natural movement belonging only to them. Two people, locked as one.

She murmured something as he thrust deep into her – a Russian expression for loving he thought – then their mouths closed on each other and they were swept away in that dance which neither ever wanted to end. Yet eventually it reached its peak in a kind of explosion and cleansing, sweeping them to the shore of some place beyond this planet, far from their previous experience.

In the sweat-soaked, pulsing, exhausting moment, their eyes locked, so they both knew that should this be the last time either was consumed in passion it did not matter, for they had tasted everything possible, good, lasting and memorable in physical love.

Later, in the afterglow, she clung to him.

'James . . . ?' Her voice husky.

'Yes?'

'On the train. When you told them to kill me, that I meant nothing to you, did you mean that?'

'Of course.'

She propped herself on one elbow and looked at him, lines of concern raking across her brow.

Then Bond laughed. 'Natalya, my darling girl, it's a basic rule. Always call their bluff.'

She grabbed a pillow and swung at him with it, almost shouting, her voice high and full of joy – 'You lying devil, James.'

He fended off the pillow and drew her back to him for a long kiss which seemed to go on until their lungs reached bursting point.

Presently, she asked him if he knew this island well.

'Why?'

'Oh, I just had a feeling that you knew where you were going when we were out driving this afternoon.'

He lay, silent for a moment. 'I know it,' he said softly. 'In some ways I have reason to hate it, but now there is a new reason for me to love it.'

'Something sad happened to you here?'

'Something I shouldn't talk about, I'm afraid.' Once more a long pause.

'There was a woman,' she said, bluntly. 'It's OK, James. I'm not jealous about what happened before we met.'

'Yes,' he heard the tiny kink in the back of his throat. 'Yes, there was a woman. She's alive, but she may never walk again. We were dealing with a very bad man.'

'As bad as Ourumov?'

'On a scale of one to ten they'd come out about equal.'

More silence and the foam surfing up the beach.

'Kiss me again, James. Please. Please take me again. Who knows what's going to happen tomorrow.'

His hands stroked her body, legs, thighs, belly, breasts, neck and shoulders. 'This is the island I really want to know,' he whispered.

'Then get to know it,' she said. 'And to hell with tomorrow.'

17

The Lake

They came in very low off the sea, crossing the coast and cruising just above the jungle. The lush greenery below looked impenetrable, but they could occasionally glimpse the odd small clearing. There was no sign of life.

'Turn ten degrees south and hold bearing one-eight-four.' Natalya had navigated all the way and brought them in right on track. She was just the kind of girl with whom Bond could have happily spent the rest of his life – smart, plenty of initiative, that sixth sense they called intuition, full of loyalty and a ferocious courage. She was not just a very attractive face and body, but a woman he could trust. In a very short time, she had come to trust him. They both knew well enough that their lives depended on each other. They also knew that, within the next few hours, they might die together.

Now, as they skimmed the deep green foliage, their heads and eyes were in constant movement as they searched for something that did not seem to be there – even though Natalya insisted it was certainly very close to where they now flew.

He caught a flicker of light some ten miles further on, and headed towards it. As they drew closer he was sure the light was that of the sun reflecting on water.

Finally there, in the middle of the jungle, was a natural bowl, a huge inland lake, its water like glass, and so deep that you could see no trace of the bottom, except at its very edges where the water lapped against a thin strip of sand, before the ground rose softly into hills of vegetation.

He turned the Piper Archer as they reached the far side of the perfect circle of water, knowing it was inconceivable that this could be nature's doing. The lake was too flawless, too geometric, to be anything but man-made.

He banked the aircraft within the bowl, one wing very low, almost reaching a rate five turn as he swung through three hundred and sixty degrees and then turned to follow through in the opposite direction.

The little plane lifted over the jungle once more.

'There's nothing there. Absolutely nothing,' Natalya said.

'Let's give it another go. I'll take her down very close to the drink. Keep your eyes peeled.'

He extended the aircraft's flaps to allow himself to fly safely at a slower speed, just over the water; curving around the complete circle, looking down on the wingtip which seemed to be only a foot or so above the smooth blue-green tint of the lake.

Still nothing. Maybe Wade was right, Bond thought. He put on power, then retracted the flaps and climbed, crossing the lake diagonally, then, after gaining height, he pulled her round again and began another run.

'James! Look out! James!' she screamed.

He saw it at exactly the same moment as she shouted. It came straight up from the deep water, breaking the placid surface with hardly a ripple, and his immediate reaction was that it was a largish fish. Now he pushed the yoke hard to the left, his feet firmly on the rudder pedals to keep the nose up in a desperate attempt to avoid what he thought was probably a 140mm rocket, and where there was one of those, more could easily follow as they usually came in distinctive seventeen rocket packs.

He had never yet heard of a launch of this type of rocket from underwater, but it would not be difficult, and the aircraft was probably being targeted electronically by computer even as he banked right, turning the Archer onto an opposite track as the first rocket passed harmlessly to their left.

'We've got to get out of here,' he shouted, slewing the plane in the other direction. Wrong! Another rocket came hurtling from the water as he turned. It did not explode, but sheared off over half the span of his port wing.

The Piper was too low and everything seemed to happen in slow motion once more. Bond over-corrected and then went out of control. He had the elevator, rudder, stabiliser and only one aileron. It was a matter of pure luck that, as he tried to correct again and bring the nose up, the belly of the aircraft struck the water.

Hitting water in any aircraft is as good as slamming into a brick wall. They went from around seventy-eight knots to zero in a fraction of a second. He felt the underside of the plane being torn away – a ragged and horrific cracking noise; then the nose went down, the prop churning water. The shore line came up to meet them and what was left of the fuselage slid up onto the sand.

Natalya had screamed when they were hit. Now, as they rose up the strip of sand, Bond threw one arm across her and his other forearm over his own face.

Then the fire gushed from the engine.

He did not recall hauling her from the wreckage, but

the next he knew was that he had carried her into the jungle foliage and had put her down gently in a clearing. Her head lolled back, then her eyelids fluttered.

He spoke her name, urgently, several times, and finally she was awake. 'You OK?'

'I think someone hit me with a hammer.' She raised herself from the ground and began to check that she could walk and move her limbs. Bond did the same. 'I think we're both in one piece.' He flexed his aching shoulders. 'Or at least the pieces appear to be joined in the right places.'

She nodded and then lost balance again, collapsing in a heap.

Bond had been vaguely aware of something else going on in the background, but was still disoriented. Now he realised that a helicopter was hovering low over the clearing, a rope snaking from it and a figure rappelling down very quickly.

At first he thought Jack Wade had been very quick off the mark in sending help. It was not until he moved towards the rope that he knew he had made a grave mistake.

A boot lashed out and caught him in the face as Xenia Onatopp reached the end of the rope to which she was secured. He managed to get halfway to his feet before she lashed out at him again. Dressed in a tight combat suit with the omnipresent machine pistol strapped to her back, Xenia was on him like a wild animal, her legs closing around his chest, knocking the wind from him and clutching, causing great stabs of pain.

'This time, Mr Bond, the pleasure will be all mine.'

His reply – 'Don't be so bloody melodramatic, Onatopp.' – was almost certainly not comprehensible as she scissored his ribs, bearing down on him.

This time she had him. He could feel the crushing, and thought the bones would crack at any minute as he fought for breath.

She started to scream orgasmically – 'Oh, yes . . . Yes . . . Yes . . .' and only stopped as an arm slid around her neck. Natalya was on her back trying to pull her from Bond, but Xenia threw her off with one arm, shouting, 'Wait for your turn. You're next.'

She had lost some of her grip in dealing with Natalya; enough for Bond to reach up behind her and get a hand around the machine pistol. His thumb hit the safety catch and he squeezed the trigger.

He had no particular purpose, but the weapon sent a spray of bullets straight up, tearing into the side of the helicopter. The pilot was obviously caught off guard for he opened up the throttle and the machine moved rapidly forward, ascending as it did so.

The line to which Xenia was secured went taut, pulling her away from Bond, who flicked her into a spin as she was lifted, at speed, across the clearing, heading straight for a tangle of tree limbs, where she was suddenly trapped in a V formation of thick branches.

Above, the helicopter was dragged backwards by the anchor of Xenia's body caught in the tree. The pilot tried to descend and regain control, but the tightness of the rope pulled the machine sideways, so that he suddenly lost it altogether. The machine tipped to one side at a dangerous angle, rapidly losing height and dropping into the trees. There was a terrible rending, then the fireball leaped up into the air.

Natalya was beside Bond as he got to his feet, rubbing at his chest, still in pain and knowing that he had been only seconds from death. He looked at Natalya, and then at Xenia's body, crushed, with her face contorted horribly in agony.

'She always did enjoy a good squeeze,' he said.

Far below the lake, in a complex similar to the one at Severnaya, Boris sat in front of a bank of monitors, his eyes riveted to one of the screens, his hands obsessively playing with a pen.

This facility, unlike Severnaya, was built in three great tiers, walkways running around each section, screens and electronics everywhere.

The monitor in front of Boris was reeling off numbers, marked as CURRENCY TRANSFERS. The figures were so large as to be almost incomprehensible. Billions of dollars were being moved from the Bank of England into a series of accounts in France, Switzerland, Brazil, Argentina, and some huge sums were even being switched into American banks.

'Going well, eh?' Alec Trevelyan stood behind him.

'And they won't know until tomorrow.'

'They will never know once we bring *Mischa* into play, my friend. What's the status? Is the satellite in range?'

Boris, looking more wild and unkempt than ever, pointed up at the long screen to his right which showed the orbit status with the red satellite symbol winking away above southern Africa.

'About six minutes.' Boris gave a little cackle.

'OK. Prepare the dish.'

Boris slapped his hand onto the console and his lower lip jutted out. 'No. Not yet. I am not ready.'

But *I am*,' Trevelyan snapped. 'I'm taking no more chances. Prepare the dish, Boris, or you won't live long enough to collect anything.'

*　　*　　*

They waited in the clearing until they both felt recovered enough to explore the lake. 'There *has* to be something here,' Bond said. 'Xenia wouldn't have tried to use her bizarre skills on us unless we were near.'

Breaking from the jungle and onto the beach, they stopped at the jaw-dropping sight in front of them. The water was moving, rippling, and from it rose three tall telescopic masts, joined together by steel cables.

'Should've come by submarine not by plane.' Bond nodded to himself.

'No wonder we didn't see anything.' Natalya had a hand up to her mouth.

Reaching their full extension, the masts locked into place. Suspended between them, exactly over the lake, they saw a latticed triangular structure with a catwalk trailing from it at a shallow angle into the water. Then the lake started to recede and, emerging from where the water had been, there came a massive parabolic shape, hundreds of feet in diameter.

'Quite a large radio dish,' Bond said.

'Is that the famous British understatement?' Natalya asked.

'Could be. Fancy climbing onto that thing? We can get up there by climbing that metal latticework.'

'After you, James.'

Far below them, inside the circular control room, Trevelyan had opened his briefcase and taken out the Golden-Eye. Holding it out to Boris, he said, 'The world's greatest cash card. I can only hope that it won't be rejected.'

Boris, watching the monitors, reported, '*Mischa* on line.'

Far away, the satellite, disguised as a piece of space junk, began to reveal itself: a silvery ULF antenna slid out, extending itself to around a distance of half a mile.

Below the so-called lake, Boris asked, 'Target co-ordinates, please.'

Trevelyan hesitated for one moment, then spoke like a commander on an electronic battlefield. 'The target is London.'

Boris started typing in sets of numbers to activate *Mischa*; and at that moment, Alec Trevelyan glanced behind him and caught sight of one of the external security screens. There he saw Bond and Natalya slowly climbing through the girders of the latticework, up onto the dish.

He sighed. 'The man just won't take a hint.' He turned to an armed uniformed guard. 'Go. Take them out before this begins to get really stupid.'

Looking up from the rim of the dish, Bond saw that the superstructure in the centre, some five hundred feet above, had begun to rotate.

'He's preparing to signal the satellite,' Natalya warned him.

'How do we stop him?'

'Look, right up there, below the superstructure, there's a maintenance room. If we can get in there, we can take out the transmitter, just above the antenna.'

Then the shooting began.

18

The Edge of Catastrophe

They could not see where the fire came from, but out there, clinging to the rim of the dish – a massive bowl where the lake had been – with the huge superstructure above its centre, they were sitting targets.

Bullets clanged into the metal around them. Natalya flinched and lost her footing on the slippery dish, slick with water and algae. Bond tried to make a grab for her and failed, losing his own balance at the same time.

They both slid down the basin, right to the centre, which was the stump of the dish, like a large blockhouse with a sealed hatch on their side. The waterproof seal, Bond guessed, could be activated from either side for there was a heavy spoked wheel in the middle. Presumably, he reasoned, there was an air lock behind the hatch for the use of any maintenance staff.

He grasped the wheel and began to turn, keeping his head down, expecting another fusillade of shots at any moment. There was a hiss as the hatch swung open, and he helped Natalya inside what appeared to be a chamber large enough to take two people. Another hatch with a wheel lay at the far end, so this had to be some kind of way in or out when the dish was below water.

A minute later, they were through the other side of the hatch, making their way down a runged ladder which, in turn, led to a pillared catwalk, circling the control room. He thought of the archives back at the Military Intelligence Headquarters. This circular control room was built on the same principle, but on a larger scale and with insulated metal, tiles and walls that held monitors, together with other complex electronics.

To their left were five or six long, high cylinders which presumably provided fuel for internal generators.

Below, on the bottom level, they could see Trevelyan and Boris seated at the firing console, and Trevelyan's voice came floating up to them – 'On my count, Boris . . .' Both men had their hands on the firing keys. 'Three . . . Two . . . One.'

They turned the keys and lights on the console started to wink from green to red. The display above read *Weapon Armed. Time to Target: 00:21:32:26.*

Natalya and Bond seemed to be rooted, horrified, to the catwalk, watching helplessly as Trevelyan uncovered the firing button and punched it, then laughed – 'God save the Queen.'

Now, with a surge of anger, Bond knew that Trevelyan had targeted England. Almost certainly London. He began to move, but Natalya caught his arm and pointed down to the middle level. A door had opened and a technician, wearing a parka with a fur hood and gloves, emerged from what they could see was a large room.

'The mainframe computer,' Natalya whispered. 'They'll have a cooling system in there. It'll be like a big refrigerator.'

She had hardly got the words out when they saw

uniformed, armed men heading up the steel staircase towards them. Bond pushed Natalya back into comparative safety behind a pillar when the section of guards began to open fire as they reached the upper level.

He fired two shots, and the first man on the catwalk spun around, grabbing air, and then the man behind him so that the pair slid back down the stairs.

Other uniformed men scrambled up the stairway and began to lay down withering fire. Bullets smashed off tiling, hit the fuel tanks or ricocheted from the walls. Bond attempted to return fire, but he was hopelessly outnumbered. He glanced round to assure himself that Natalya was all right, but she had gone. He peered around and thought he saw a figure somewhere below the catwalk, dangling and moving hand over hand directly underneath.

Natalya had quietly run from behind the pillar, taken a peep at the underside of the catwalk and seen that a series of rungs ran directly along it. Now she was hanging from them, reaching out and grabbing, moving from rung to rung, heading towards the door that led to the mainframe computer room.

Staying as close as he could to the wall, Bond ducked behind the first long fuel tank, slid his hand into a pouch on his belt and drew out one of the small magnetic mines Q had sent in the briefcase. Fuel was dripping from the bullet holes, and he dodged back, loosing off another couple of rounds, then attaching a mine to the next tank. He continued, firing and retreating, giving himself time to place the electronically controlled mines under the tanks.

This continued until Bond realised that his pistol was empty and he would have to take the chance that Natalya was about to do something very constructive. Hopelessly outnumbered, he threw his automatic out onto the walkway, placed his hands above his head and walked out to face the knot of troops, hoping they at least had the discipline to cease firing.

As he moved out, he caught a glimpse of Natalya dropping from the underside of the catwalk and landing by the door which led into the mainframe computer room. He took his eyes from her for a second and faced his captors. When he glanced down again, she had disappeared.

Her breath immediately condensed in the freezing atmosphere of the mainframe room. Natalya glanced around. Without protective clothing she could only last for a few minutes in this place, so she hurried over to the long plastic keyboard, grabbing at the chair set in front of it. Immediately her fingers touched the metal on the chair they froze and she had to pull them off, ripping skin from her hand as she did so.

Behind her she glimpsed the large stainless steel vats, each bearing the international *Do Not Touch* symbol with a −200° mark. Liquid nitrogen, she thought, the coolant for the mainframe, keeping it at a steady, very low temperature.

Carefully, Natalya seated herself at the plastic keyboard and began to work.

On the highest walkway, the section of troops to whom Bond had surrendered were frisking him: making him lean with his hands flat against the wall. From this position, he could clearly see the mines he had set under the fuel tanks, their little red lights winking to show they were armed and would detonate once he used the watch on his left wrist. He tried to distract the men patting him down by keeping up a stream of abuse and turning his head away from the tanks.

They found no further weapons on him, so eventually Bond was frog-marched down the two flights of steel stairs and up to the console where Trevelyan worked with Boris.

'James!' Trevelyan turned in his chair, speaking in almost a jovial manner. 'What a damned unpleasant surprise.'

'I always aim to please, Alec.'

Trevelyan raised an eyebrow. 'I suppose that's the difference between us. I aim to kill.' His eyes hardened. 'Where's the girl?'

'We're not seeing each other right now.'

'Really? My people said she was with you.' He turned to the guards. 'Find her. She has to be in here somewhere.'

Two of the men left quickly, the other two remained with Bond, placing the contents of his pockets on the console in front of Trevelyan. As they did so, Bond carefully scanned the monitors. He took in the long scrolling line of transfers from the Bank of England to various banks throughout the world. Then he felt his stomach lurch as he saw the global screen with satellite *Mischa* over Spain, on a direct course for London. The countdown clock kept going, standing at the moment at *TIME TO TARGET 00:15:07:39*. He had around a quarter of an hour to stop what would undoubtedly be the greatest catastrophe ever to befall his country. With this kind of urgency, there was only one thing he could do. Without being too obvious about it, he let his right hand drift over to his left wrist. If he activated the mines under the fuel tanks, everyone would die and the satellite would eventually drift down and burn out without firing its nuclear bomb to produce an electronic pulse of the capital.

He took in the fact that an elevator stood, with doors open, to the far left of the console, next to a technician who was monitoring the guidance system.

Trevelyan was sorting through the pocket litter on the console. Keys, money clip, pen, coins. He gave the pen a quick examination, even clicking it once, scribbling with it on a pad before clicking it off again. Bond was relieved when he put the pen back on the console. A few more clicks and he would not even have time to activate the mines.

Trevelyan's hand suddenly shot up to Bond's left arm. 'The watch please, James,' yanking it from his wrist, then examining it with an indulgent smile. 'How is old Q doing these days? Up to his usual tricks, I suppose. I see you have the new model.' Slowly he turned it over to reveal a tiny red pinpoint winking on the underside. 'I still press here, do I?' He pressed the stem and then the small button to the right. The red light immediately stopped winking, and Bond knew that the arming devices in the mines themselves would also blink off and revert to their deactivated mode. He wondered how much fuel was still leaking from the tanks and reckoned that it would be a fair amount – running down the catwalk, dripping all the way down to this, the lowest level.

In the mainframe computer room, Natalya, shivering with cold, typed as rapidly as she could and had all but completed her instructions when the two guards burst in on her. She managed to hit the *Enter* key, banging it hard, before they dragged her from the chair and led her off, down the stairs to where Bond stood under guard, and Trevelyan sat smiling happily. Boris continued with his work on the keyboard. Above, the global screen showed *Mischa* gradually moving closer to its target, and Bond looked from the screen to Natalya being brought across the floor. To his pleasure he saw the guards' boots left damp stains as they marched towards him. The fuel must be spreading both ways.

Before the little party reached the console area, Bond relaxed. 'Interesting little set-up you have here, Alec. I see that you break into the bank via computer and then make certain large sums of money are transferred – I presume just seconds before you activate GoldenEye which, of course, erases all records of transactions, together with the entire target. Very ingenious.'

'Thank you, James. High praise indeed, coming from you.'

Bond gestured with his head. 'Still nothing but petty theft, Alec. In the end you're nothing more than a bank robber. A common thief. A common murderer also.'

'Hardly, James. You always did have a small mind. You see, it's not just a question of bank records.' His eyes, now like a stormy sky, scanned Bond's face. 'It's everything in every computer in greater London. Tax records. The stock market. Credit ratings, land registries. Even criminal records . . .' He looked up at the countdown clock. 'In eleven minutes and forty-three – no two . . . one – seconds, the United Kingdom will once more enter the Stone Age.'

'Followed by Tokyo, Frankfurt, New York, Hong Kong. A world-wide financial meltdown.' He looked as though he pitied Trevelyan. 'All so that mad little Alec can settle a score with the world fifty years on. So you can settle an injustice done to your ancestors.'

'Oh, please, James, spare me any Freudian analysis. I might as well ask you if all those vodka martinis ever silence the screams of all the men and women you've killed . . .' He looked past Bond to the guards bringing Natalya towards them. '. . . Or do you find your forgiveness in the arms of all those willing women?' He slammed his hand hard onto the console. 'England is about to learn the final cost of betrayal.'

Natalya had been brought close to them now. 'Welcome to the party, my dear Natalya.'

Boris, hearing her name, swivelled his chair and saw her. 'Natalya?' He sounded shocked.

'This isn't just one of your games, Boris. Real people are about to die, you contemptuous little bastard.' She shrugged free of her captors and took a step forward, her palm hitting him hard on the left cheek and then a backhander to the right.

They roughly pulled her back and, in the tiny skirmish, the pen, given to Bond by Q, rolled onto the floor. Boris slowly reached down, picked it up and began to click it on and off.

Bond watched him, fascinated by the clicks. 'Click-click' one more and the device would be armed. But Boris merely started to roll the pen between his fingers.

'Where did you find her?' Trevelyan asked her guards.

'She was in the mainframe, sir.'

Trevelyan scowled, then snapped at Boris, 'Check the programme.'

Boris chuckled. 'She couldn't put a bug in a simple game, let alone damage us. She's a moron. A second level programmer. Anyway, she doesn't have access to the firing codes. All she knows about is the guidance system.' As he said it, Boris seemed to slow down, slurring the final words and, at that moment, an alarm began to beep, as though someone had tried to break into a car.

A technician, sitting at the far monitor, all but shouted, 'Retro-rockets firing.'

It was time for Natalya to smile, but Bond kept his eyes on Boris who now resumed clicking the pen. Three – the pen was armed. A further three times, disarming the pen.

Boris leaped across to the technician: hammering at the keyboard with his right hand. 'She's at ninety-seven miles and falling. I can't regain control.'

'What the hell's going on?' Trevelyan was up on his feet

and moving towards Boris and the technician who looked bewildered.

'We'll have re-entry in thirteen minutes,' as he reached forward to set a re-entry clock. The timer flashed on in brilliant red digitised figures, and the *Time to Target* now read, *Aborted. Time To Re-entry: 13:24.*

In the stunned silence, Natalya spoke. 'It's going to burn up somewhere over the Atlantic.'

'You little bitch.' Boris was still trying to regain control from the technician's keyboard. He moved his head up to speak with Trevelyan. 'She's changed the access codes.'

As he spoke, Trevelyan, his face a rage, pulled his gun and stuck it in Boris' ear.

Natalya giggled. 'Go ahead, Janus. Shoot him, he means nothing to me.'

Bond gave her a look of pleasure and muttered, 'Standard operating procedure.'

'I can break her codes, move that damned gun away, Alec.' Boris flapped at the pistol as though it were an insect, then turned back to the technician. 'Load the guidance sub-routines. Now. Quickly.' Then he started playing with the pen again.

Click-click

Click-click

Then a whole series of clicks so that Bond lost count, just as Trevelyan took his pistol from Boris' ear and turned it onto Natalya. 'Tell him. You hear me, girl? Tell him.'

Boris was out of control, whirling and screaming at Natalya, 'Give me those codes. Natalya, GIVE ME THE CODES.'

Bond had no idea of the status of the pen that the crazy little computer specialist was waving in Natalya's face. He lashed out with one arm, sending Trevelyan's gun up and out of the man's hand. He then brought his foot up in a kick boxer's stance, kicking Boris' wrist and sending the pen arcing into the air. For a precious second it seemed to remain stationary in mid air, then dropped, exploding just as it hit the spreading pool of fuel.

The explosion and sudden leap of fire around them made hands and arms come up: all trying to cover their eyes from the sheet of flame which shot up the stairs and wall back to its original source.

The first fuel tank exploded. As it did so, Bond grabbed Natalya by the arm and pulled her towards the elevator on their left. As he banged the door closed, they both almost felt the thud of bullets hitting the sliding doors.

'Can he really break your codes?' Bond asked. He was aware of the urgency in his own voice.

'It's possible,' she said almost casually.

'Then we'll have to destroy the transmitter.' His head tilted up, watching the numbers rise. He could only presume this would take them right to the top of the damned thing.

'That would be natural.' She lifted one eyebrow. 'By the way, thank you, I'm fine.'

'Good.'

The elevator stopped at the base of the catwalk which led to the transmitter cradle they had seen as the whole structure rose from the lake. An armed guard turned towards the opening doors and saw the woman slumped on the floor. He immediately ran in to her, dropping his machine pistol on the way in his hurry to help her. As he began to kneel down beside the unconscious body, Bond dropped from the roof, where he had lodged himself, using shoulders and feet, like a climber in a chimney rock formation.

First his feet hit the guard's back, then he chopped

viciously at the man's neck which gave off a horrible cracking sound as he fell, spread-eagled, to the floor.

Natalya was on her feet again as Bond removed the
guard's pistol and threw it to her. He picked up the
machine pistol, and, as he did so, they both heard
the rumbling of explosions from far below.

'You know how to use one of these?' Looking at the
gun he had handed to Natalya.

She nodded, checking the slide movement, ejecting the
magazine and making sure it was full. 'Yes,' she said.

'Good. Just keep out of sight and get off the dish. I'm
going to scupper that antenna. That *will* do the trick, won't
it?'

'Just get up there to the maintenance hatch. There's
probably a simple chain device which works the mechanism to turn the antenna. The best thing for you to do is
remove all the fuses from the maintenance room. Go. Go
now. Quickly.'

From below, more explosions rattled the dish and the
superstructure as Bond kissed her on the cheek and started
the long climb up to the maintenance room high above
the antenna.

19

Journeys End in Lovers Meeting

The climb was daunting, and by the time Bond reached halfway, he could make out the structures more clearly. When he was some forty feet up, he glanced down and saw Natalya making a dash up to the edge of the dish, climbing over the latticework to the ground and running into the protection of the jungle.

Originally he had intended to stop at the catwalk which crossed the triangle some ten feet above the big metal maintenance room which, in turn, was set directly above the housing from which the long icicle of the antenna reached down, ending around ten feet from the dish. Now he saw that there was another large chamber, high above, set into the very apex of the triangle. Cables and wires sprouted downwards from this room, and he began to get the whole picture of how the antenna was operated.

The wires and cables, leading from the top of the triangle, undoubtedly had a part to play in the way the great silver finger was moved. Some went directly down, through the maintenance chamber and from there into what could only be the true mechanism for repositioning the antenna, yet there seemed to be another set of thicker cables. These went over a series of pulleys and wheels.

He was thirty feet from the top of the structure when he saw that these wires ran to the far side of the dish and supported a cable car which could be taken from dish level up to the catwalk.

He cursed, wishing he had known about the cable car for it would have cut precious minutes off his journey.

From far below, he still caught the sound of occasional explosions coming from deep within the earth beyond the dish.

In the control complex, the fuel tanks were still exploding, sending balls of fire up to the roof above the top section. Guards raced back and forth with CO_2 extinguishers, but nobody was in doubt that the roof was starting to weaken. Tiles and pieces of insulation had already begun to fall, and Trevelyan's men kept their eyes on this danger point, as though trying to divine the moment when they would have to give up and evacuate the complex.

The only person who seemed oblivious to the dangers was Boris who sat at his keyboard, focused wholly on the job of regaining control over the satellite.

Trevelyan stood over him, watching his every move as the younger man worked, almost feverishly, at the programme.

'How long's it going to take?' Trevelyan was looking around and starting to take in the possible hopelessness of the situation.

Boris snapped back that it was nearly done. 'Two minutes . . . three at the most.'

Trevelyan suddenly frowned, remembering Bond who could blow out the all important antenna if he had a mind to. If he knew Q, and if Bond still had explosives with him, he might find a way of overriding the electronic remotes. He turned to the guard who was standing beside him. 'Watch him,' he pointed to Boris. 'If he moves, shoot him.'

He was away and running towards the exit, pushing firefighters out of the way, heading for the cable car that would take him as far as the catwalk above the maintenance room.

Within a couple of minutes he was in the little cage and beginning his slow ascent up the structure.

In front of Boris the countdown clock read *Time to Re-entry: 09:41*.

As Trevelyan began the journey to the catwalk, so Bond had reached the chamber at the top of the framework.

It had been fashioned into a square, metal room, and Bond was forced to move carefully between two different sets of machinery. On one side, he could see, there was a series of large, cogged wheels around which cables ran out and downwards. As he entered, the wheels began to move, the mechanism starting up. Someone was in the cable car, which meant he had little time left.

Immediately beside the door was a great oblong structure which pulsed with sound. There seemed to be no way into it, but it did not take much imagination for Bond to realise that this was the generator and probably the first stage in controlling the antenna.

During the climb, he had already thought of trying to use the last of Q's mines. These were strictly remote controlled units, but there was a way he could set them on a timer. His real problem was that the timer could only be set to detonate the mine with a five-minute delay.

He pulled the black circular object from his pouch, together with a small screwdriver, and began to release the screws on the underside. He worked calmly. When dealing with explosives he knew there were inherent dangers in rushing things.

Halfway through the process, the cable car mechanism stopped with a lurch. Whoever was in the car had already reached the catwalk.

Inside the mine, he removed the remote timer – a small microchip the size of his thumbnail. Below it was a small dial with a moving pointer like the large hand on a watch. Using the screwdriver he carefully turned the pointer, swinging it around to its furthest setting. The mechanism began to click as the pointer slowly moved backwards. Placing the mine below the generator, he swung himself out of the room, preparing to make the climb down to the catwalk.

He had descended three rungs when two bullets whined past him. In one movement, Bond slid the machine pistol from his shoulder and looked down.

Trevelyan stood in the middle of the catwalk, his right hand holding an automatic pistol, raised, ready to take another shot.

Turning to the inside of the structure, Bond fired a fast, unaimed burst in Trevelyan's direction. The shots went wide, but Trevelyan ducked, throwing himself to the end of the catwalk nearest the small cage which was the cable car.

Bond scrambled down and fired another burst. He could see sparks shooting off the metal, but his target had disappeared. The catwalk was now only around twelve feet below him. He hesitated for a second, which almost cost him his life, for two more shots came from the direction of the cable car, whanging against the metal near his head. Swinging inside the triangular lines and girders, Bond pushed off and dropped to the catwalk which began to sway crazily as he landed, firing a long burst into the cable car.

It took a second for him to realise that the car was empty, and he turned just in time to see that Trevelyan had somehow worked his way to the other side of the catwalk, and so positioned himself behind him.

The man who was Janus gave a smile of pleasure as he raised the automatic.

'Goodbye, James,' he mouthed, and squeezed the trigger. The firing pin came down with a click that Bond seemed to hear as though it were amplified in an echo chamber. Trevelyan shouted an oath and flung the empty pistol straight at Bond who had already raised his weapon, bringing it to bear.

The pistol grazed the side of his head, knocking him to one side, just as he fired. The burst went wide. It also ended with a loud click and the mechanism of the gun locked. He was also out of ammunition.

Slightly dizzy from the blow, he barely had time to dodge as Trevelyan rushed him. He side-stepped and brought his fist up, aiming at his one-time friend's jaw.

The blow connected with the side of Trevelyan's head and sent him sprawling and rolling over the catwalk.

Bond looked down, seeing that it was a ten-foot drop to the top of the maintenance room below. This time he did not hesitate, but vaulted over the catwalk, landing heavily on the roof.

He scrambled to one side, and let himself down to the entrance. As he climbed in, there was a whining sound and the whir of an electric motor. Someone was repositioning the antenna.

Down under the earth, Boris was making wild war whoops, almost dancing around, shouting, 'I've done it.

Yes. I am invincible!' as he typed the final command –
SEND COMMAND: ABORT RE-ENTRY.

The countdown clock read *Re-entry: 07:45*.

Then the screen cleared and scrolled out the message.
STANDBY: ANTENNA REPOSITIONING.

The sound Bond heard in the maintenance room was that
of the mechanism beginning to operate and reset the co-
ordinates, swinging the long, tapering spike of the antenna
to the correct point to regain control of the satellite. He
looked around, searching for a fuse box of some kind, but
all the equipment in the maintenance chamber was sealed:
a large grey metal box took up most of the space, and cables
originating from the mechanism in the apex of the structure
were encased in protective plastic covers.

As he stood, searching for a way to deal with the electronics, a heavy thud shook the whole room, leaving him
in no doubt that Trevelyan had also leaped down from
the catwalk.

He expected the mine to detonate at any minute now,
but that could fail and he still wanted to make certain the
antenna did not aim itself correctly. Outside, he looked
down and dropped, landing on the housing that he knew
contained the final stage of the mechanism.

There was a hatch into this great circular housing, and
he was quickly inside, knowing that Trevelyan was at his
heels.

There was little room, for a huge wheel like that of
some great clock took up the bulk of the space. But he
spotted two other things immediately – a long, oblong
fuse box and a telescopic ladder, attached to the wall and
directly above a steel trapdoor. This, he was sure, would
be the way the engineers were able to get right down to
the antenna. He also knew that from this point to the dish
itself there were some eighty or ninety feet.

As his mind raced, so he unscrewed the butterfly bolts on the fuse box, flipped it open and began smashing the fuses out in groups of five and six at a time until they were all gone and the whir of machinery stopped.

Trevelyn was close now, he could almost smell the man, just as he could smell his own fear. Leaping towards the telescopic ladder, he unclipped the safety bolts to allow it to fall.

As Trevelyan appeared in the hatchway, so Bond stamped hard on the trapdoor, his hands on the bottom rung of the ladder.

The trapdoor gave way and the ladder uncoiled, ratchetting down through some forty feet and coming to a sickening halt at its fullest extension only a few feet above the top of the antenna.

He thought his arms were about to be ripped from their sockets, but he held on grimly, the ladder swaying and creaking above him as Trevelyan's face appeared in the trapdoor.

'Need some help getting down, James?' he shouted. 'I'll be with you in a minute.' Easing himself through the opening, Trevelyan began to make a slow descent as Bond attempted uselessly to pull himself back up the ladder.

Natalya moved into the jungle following the noise she had just heard. She had no desire to look at what she had seen from the edge of the thick trees and fronds – James struggling at the end of a long swinging ladder, some forty feet from the bottom of the dish and directly above the antenna. She moved slowly towards the noise, and came to a halt as she reached a man-made clearing. In the middle of this glade stood a helicopter gunship, its rotors gently idling.

*   *   *

Below ground, in the control complex, Boris stared unbelieving at the screen which now read out, ANTENNA MALFUNCTION. He began to scream and stamp, yelling unintelligible obscenities.

Above Bond, the ladder was swaying as Trevelyan came down, rung by rung. Two rungs above Bond, he took one hand from the ladder and pulled a small throat microphone from inside his shirt, speaking into it rapidly.

In the jungle clearing, Natalya saw the pilot alone in the cockpit. The helicopter gunship began to move, its engine spooling up, ready to lift off. Taking a deep breath, she ran towards the rear door of the machine.

'Now, James, it's time for our last goodbye, I think.' Trevelyan stepped down to the rung directly above Bond and raised his booted foot to bring it down on Bond's hand. As he did so, the rung gave way with a sharp crack.

He felt Trevelyan's body brush against his as he dropped. In a reflex, he grabbed with one hand and caught Trevelyan's left wrist.

The man looked up at him, sweat and terror on his face. 'James,' he called, his eyes pleading. 'Haul me up. For heaven's sake . . . for old times' sake, haul me up.'

'Go to hell!' Bond shouted and released Trevelyan who hit the antenna and, screaming, dropped all the way down to the dish.

At the same moment the apex of the triangle blew out. The mine had detonated, and the entire structure swayed, pieces of metal and wiring beginning to detach themselves and fall.

Over the noise, Bond thought he could hear a helicopter. Hanging precariously, he saw the gunship, heading straight for him, and as it hovered as near as was feasible, his eyes widened.

The pilot was manoeuvring the gunship closer and closer. Behind him, Natalya stood with her pistol pushed into the side of the terrified man's head. He was acting under her instructions, which, because of the skeletal edifice they were approaching, were not always practical.

After a minute's jigging from side to side, he brought the craft's port landing skid to a point just in front and below where Bond hung. It was his only chance, for everything appeared to be collapsing around him. He swung himself out and grabbed hold of the skid at the moment the chopper backed off and started to move away.

In the centre of the dish, Trevelyan regained consciousness. His eyes opened and the pain that swept over him, combined with the blood in his mouth, told him that he was near death.

He heard the noises coming from above, cracks, creaks, the clank of falling metal. Looking up, the last thing he saw was the long silver spike that was the antenna detach itself and come hurtling down to impale him.

In the control complex, Boris still raved, but realised that most of the guards were either dead or had disappeared. He seemed to be the only one left alive, and he rushed up to the middle gallery. As he reached the mainframe room, so the liquid coolants suddenly exploded, sending a freezing white mist flying through the shuttered doors.

For a second, Boris knew what was happening as the mist enveloped him, then he felt himself seizing up. After that he died, standing, a frozen statue inside the doomed building.

* * *

The gunship came down gently into the clearing. Bond dropped thankfully to the ground and stretched out, his eyes closed.

Inside, Natalya spoke in rapid Russian, telling the pilot that if he tried no tricks, he could leave, then she ran back and jumped from the main door onto the earth next to Bond.

The gunship, with a thankful pilot at the controls, lifted off as she spoke softly. 'James . . . ? James . . . ? Are you OK? James, oh please speak to me.'

He opened one eye and pulled her down to him. 'Yes,' he said. 'I'm fine. Thank you.'

'You devil,' she laughed and he pulled her close so that their mouths touched and he rolled on top of her.

'James, no. Not here, James, somebody might see.'

'Don't be silly, Natalya.' He looked at her lovingly. 'There's nobody left to see anything.'

He only had eyes for Natalya, so could not see Jack Wade rise from the bushes, nor the forty or so marines, in camouflage, appear from the jungle to stand smiling with pleasure.

From far away came the sound of Marine Cougar helicopters bringing in reinforcements.

Bond needed no backup at this particular time.